W9-BSP-344

He Kissed Her With The Skill That Had Slain Her Resistance From The Start.

Xavier's tongue traced the seam of Megan's lips. Teasing her. Tempting her. Coaxing a response from her that she didn't want to give.

She opened her mouth and let him in. His familiar taste overwhelmed her, and she couldn't resist moving closer for one final delicious press of his body against hers.

His arms surrounded her, banding her against his muscled length, and his heat seeped into her, melting her resistance, warming her for the first time since she'd left him. She clutched his waist, caressed his strong back. Being with him like this felt so good, so right.

Saying goodbye shouldn't be this hard.

* * *

EMILIE ROSE

THE PRICE OF HONOR

ISBN-13: 978-0-373-73137-4

THE PRICE OF HONOR

Books by Emilie Rose

Harlequin Desire

Her Tycoon to Tame #2112
The Price of Honor #2124

Silhouette Desire

Forbidden Passion #1624
Breathless Passion #1635
Scandalous Passion #1660
Condition of Marriage #1675
*Paying the Playboy's Price #1732
*Exposing the Executive's Secrets #1738
*Bending to the Bachelor's Will #1744
Forbidden Merger #1753
†The Millionaire's Indecent Proposal #1804
†The Prince's Ultimate Deception #1810
†The Playboy's Passionate Pursuit #1817
††Secrets of the Tycoon's Bride #1831
**Shattered by the CEO #1871
**Bound by the Kincaid Baby #1881
**Wed by Deception #1894
Pregnant on the Upper East Side? #1903
Bargained Into Her Boss's Bed #1934
‡More Than a Millionaire #1963
‡Bedding the Secret Heiress #1973
‡His High-Stakes Holiday Seduction #1980
Executive's Pregnancy Ultimatum #1994
Wedding His Takeover Target #2048

*Trust Fund Affairs
†Monte Carlo Affairs
††The Garrisons
**The Payback Affairs
‡The Hightower Affairs

All backlist available in ebook

EMILIE ROSE

Bestselling Harlequin Desire author and RITA® Award finalist Emilie Rose lives in her native North Carolina with her four sons and two adopted mutts. Writing is her third (and hopefully her last) career. She's managed a medical office and run a home day care, neither of which offers half as much satisfaction as plotting happy endings. Her hobbies include gardening and cooking (especially cheesecake). She's a rabid country music fan because she can find an entire book in almost any song. She is currently working her way through her own "bucket list," which includes learning to ride a Harley. Visit her website at www.emilierose.com or email EmilieRoseC@aol.com. Letters can be mailed to P.O. Box 20145, Raleigh, NC 27619.

To my mom who battled back from the brink of death
this year for me and my boys.
I don't know what we'd do without her.
Love you, Mom.

And to the man upstairs
for giving me more time with my mom.

One

"The tabloids are at it again." Megan Sutherland dropped the newspaper on the kitchen table in front of Xavier, and then because she couldn't resist, she bent and hugged him from behind, reveling in the warmth of his neck against her lips, his subtle custom-blended cologne, the firm pecs beneath her fingertips and the thick dark hair tickling her cheek.

As always, his nearness sent a shimmer of happiness through her. Love swelled in her chest and hunger settled heavily in her womb. One of these days the words she fought so hard to contain were going to burst free, but today she bit her tongue because he wasn't ready to hear them. Nor was he ready to hear her news.

A sobering thought. She forced herself to back away and head for the coffeepot to get a jump start on the chaotic day she had scheduled.

"Give a guy a few million bucks and a perfume empire

and the tabloid reporters get creative. Funny, isn't it?" she
called over her shoulder and waited for the sexy chuckle
that never failed to make her knees weak. But the kitchen
remained silent as she filled her cup. Eerily silent.

Surprised, she turned. "Did you hear what I said?"

"I heard." His tight voice and the intent look on his face
as he stared at the folded page made her pulse flutter. Then
his gaze met hers. The resolve in his green eyes filled her
stomach with lead.

"They're lying. Aren't they, Xavier?" Her last words,
forced through a tightening throat, sounded a bit strident.

"No."

Dizziness swamped her. Her fingers stung. She looked
down to see hot coffee sloshing over the rim of the delicate
china and dripping to the floor. She set the cup on the
counter, grabbed a towel and bent to mop up the mess,
taking a moment to gather her composure. She probably
shouldn't be drinking coffee anyway, but until the doctor
confirmed—

No. She knew without a doubt that she carried Xavier's
baby.

She slowly rose on rubbery legs. "But the article says
the blonde is your fiancée, that you're marrying her one
year from today."

"That is correct."

Megan's body went numb, paralyzed with shock. It took
several seconds before she could wheeze air into her lungs.
"What about us?"

"This has nothing to do with our relationship, Megan.
My pending marriage has been arranged for years."

Feeling slowly returned to her limbs as though icicles
were splintering through her veins in painful shards.
"Years?" she squeaked. "You've been engaged for *years*?
And you didn't tell me?"

"It was irrelevant. Our affair was never intended to be anything other than casual. You knew that."

Casual. Being crushed beneath a falling horse would hurt less. "I know in the beginning we agreed no strings. But…"

Sometime over the past six months she'd fallen in love with Xavier Alexandre, with his old-fashioned manners, his worldly sophistication and his second-to-none bedroom skills. And now she wanted more than just an affair to remember. She wanted forever. With him. She'd believed he felt the same since he spent every free moment with her.

"There is no 'but.' It is my duty to marry Cecille."

Cecille. Hearing her name from his lips was like the crack of a bullwhip.

"Do you love her?" *Don't ask if you don't want to know.* Dread over his response tensed her abdominal muscles.

"My feelings are not important."

"They are to me."

"It is a business transaction. Nothing more."

A business transaction. How could the most passionate man she'd ever encountered sound so emotionless about something as important, as *intimate,* as marriage? "Are you sleeping with her?"

"Megan, this need not concern you."

"Need not concern me! Since you've been in my bed almost every night for the past six months, I think I have a right to know if you're sleeping with someone else. Are you?"

"I have had no other women since I met you. Does that please you, *ma petite concourante?*"

His little competitor. She used to love it when he called her that. But it didn't make her smile now. She should be comforted by his admission that he hadn't been hopping from her bed to this blonde woman's. But it wasn't enough.

"You're going to go through with it, then? The marriage?"

"It is a matter of honor."

"Honor? Where was your honor when you were making me believe we had a future together that involved more than me riding you and your horses?"

His eyebrows slammed downward in a formidable scowl. "Have I ever made promises to you that I did not keep?"

"No. But I thought…" She twisted the towel in her hands. "I *hoped* you and I would get married. Eventually. And have a family."

"Did I not tell you in the beginning that I would never offer marriage?"

With pain choking her, she couldn't force a word out. She could only nod.

"And I will not have an illegitimate child. That is why we have always used protection."

But she couldn't tolerate birth control pills and condoms weren't fail-proof, as she'd learned firsthand. She fought the urge to shield her tummy. He had a child on the way. He just didn't know it yet. She'd only put the clues together yesterday and taken the pregnancy test this morning before her run. She'd been planning to tell him tonight during an intimate dinner for two. When she found the right words.

But everything had changed now, and there were no words that could make this situation right. Not if he was going to marry someone else.

Her pride gave her a kick in the pants. "Well, forgive me for getting the impression you might have reconsidered when you bought this house bordering your estate and set me up in it. And when you've followed me to every city on the Grand Prix circuit so you could share my bed."

"And to watch you ride my horses—three very expensive investments. I have enjoyed our time together, Megan, and will continue to savor each moment we share until the very last."

"When you leave me for her." Indignation prickled her scalp. "Your fiancée might have something to say about that."

"She has no say in my private affairs before the wedding. As I have stated, the marriage is a business arrangement. Neither Cecille nor I are going into this with any illusions of something as transient as love."

Megan's love didn't feel transient at all. It felt like a big gaping hole in her heart—one that would follow her to the grave.

Xavier folded his napkin with crisp precision, rose and approached her. She couldn't bear to look at his aristocratically handsome face. More specifically, she couldn't handle the absence of the warmth and tenderness that were usually in his beautiful emerald eyes when he focused on her. At that moment he looked every inch the ruthless businessman he was rumored to be. Certainly not the man she'd believed—mistakenly, apparently—had fallen in love with her, the man who treated her like she was someone precious and wonderful and who didn't expect her to change one iota of her person to be with him.

An immaculately fitted Italian suit outlined his lean, tall form and the powerful muscles he conditioned when they worked out side by side in the gym he'd installed in the spare bedroom for her. He had already dressed to board the helicopter that would fly him to Parfums Alexandre's corporate offices in Nice the moment she left for the stables on his estate. No traffic jams for him. He simply flew over them all and landed on the roof of his office building.

Only this time when he left she wouldn't spend the hours eagerly awaiting his return or daydreaming of the sensual delights they'd share in bed tonight. Instead she'd be worrying about whether he was with *her*. The woman he intended to marry. The woman who wasn't casual or temporary.

He released an exasperated breath. "Megan, there is no need to be melodramatic. Our relationship will continue unchanged. We will have the next twelve months together."

"You expect me to sleep with you while you're engaged to someone else?" The idea seemed unconscionable. "And then what? You'll marry her? And forget all about me? About us and what we've shared? Like discarding an out-of-style suit?"

"I will never forget you, *mon amante*." He lifted his hand toward her cheek.

The gentle stroke of his fingertips made her shiver. Unable to stomach her traitorous body's response, she backed up a step. Inhaling slowly, then exhaling, she willed the fuzzy-headed this-can't-be-happening feeling away and tried to gather her thoughts.

"What if I asked you to choose between her and me?"

"Don't."

The inflexible word crushed her hopes and dreams. The idea of her man—the one she adored immeasurably—making love to her while planning to marry someone else made her want to howl and throw things. And she wasn't the tantrum-throwing type. He might as well rip out her heart and grind it beneath his custom-made Italian shoes.

She would not be the other woman. She would not beg for his attention or settle for the crumbs his wife allowed him to toss her way.

And what about the baby she carried?

What of her career?

Her home?

Everything she'd counted on had been completely upset by his engagement. Panic clawed at her. She needed to think, to plan, to try to find a way out of this mess, and she couldn't do that with Xavier watching her.

She tossed the towel aside. "I have to get to the stables."

"Megan—"

"I can't talk to you about this right now. I have horses and clients waiting for me."

"Tonight, then."

She barely managed not to snort in disbelief. Did he honestly believe she'd come home after work and *casually* share dinner the way they always did? Dinner. Then bed. Then lie in his arms all night and think about *her?* No way.

She raced into the bedroom. The fact that he didn't come after her spoke volumes. She shed her running clothes and yanked on her riding attire. Her hair was damp and she probably reeked of sweat from her run, but she didn't care. A shower was the least of her worries. She stomped into her boots.

Her cell phone blinked on its charger, indicating a new voice mail message. Unable to deal with whoever had called now, she snatched up the device and shoved it into her jacket pocket without checking caller ID.

She bolted from what until this morning had been her paradise, a fairy-tale cottage, part of the fairy-tale life she and Xavier had created. She heard the helicopter's blades in the distance. Xavier had already left, as if this day— the one where he'd shattered her dreams and wrecked her life—were as routine as any other.

She'd sprinted half the distance to the stable before stopping beneath a tree—and out of sight of the rising chopper—to gather her shattered control. Struggling to catch her breath, she leaned against the rough bark and wiped the moisture from her face. Tears, not sweat. And she never cried. *Never.* Tears were useless and they never fixed anything. But, damn him, Xavier had driven her to tears for the first time since hearing about the plane crash that had killed her family.

She took big gulping breaths, but she couldn't seem to stem the flow. She was pregnant. And the only man she'd ever allowed herself to love, the father of her baby, was going to marry someone else.

He had made it clear he wouldn't want this child.

Do you?

Given the circumstances—the *new* circumstances—she didn't know.

Part of her relished the idea of holding the proof of her love for Xavier in her arms. But her logical side argued that children and the Grand Prix circuit were not a winning combination. Only a few riders juggled parenthood and competition successfully, and they did so with the help of nannies and understanding spouses. Could she make it work without Xavier's help?

She worked crazy long hours, often seven days a week, and the travel was grueling. What kind of mother could she be with that schedule? Her child would suffer without a second parent to fill the gaps. Single parenthood would be nothing like the merry band of gypsies she, her brother, mother and father had been before the crash.

Continuing the pregnancy would be incredibly complicated. Even if she booted Xavier's gorgeous butt and his horses to the curb, how would she hide her condition from him if she stayed on the continent? She was almost two months pregnant and it wouldn't be long before she'd start to show.

Would he try to talk her into an abortion or fight her for custody on principle? This was Xavier's baby, and what Xavier owned Xavier kept. Would he feel as territorial about an unplanned love child?

It didn't matter. Megan wouldn't risk having her child

raised by his wife—someone who might not want it, love and cherish it. Someone who might resent the hell out of the onerous duty thrust upon her.

Been there. Done that. After her family had been killed, her childhood hadn't been the greeting card kind. Even though her uncle had taken her in, he'd made sure she always knew she was an unwelcome burden. An outsider. *That woman's* child.

And what about her cottage—the house Xavier had bought for her? Even if he'd let her, she couldn't stay there after he married someone else. Especially since her place had a clear view of the driveway to his estate. She'd see his wife coming and going. And that would destroy her.

She bent over double, hands on her knees. *What are you going to do?*

Panic tightened like a noose around her neck. She had to focus on the present rather than worry about what might happen months from now. *Deal with today. Then the rest.*

The birth control failure couldn't have come at a worse time. She was on the verge of realizing her dream of making it to the top as a Grand Prix rider and trainer on the European circuit. Not only were her horses racking up credentials, but she'd been signing more and more exclusive clients each season. She rode over a dozen horses any given day. And she had a reputation for being the "go-to" girl when a rider sustained an injury and needed a temporary replacement.

But she couldn't do any of that while she was expecting. Taking time off for a pregnancy would mean losing ranking and income from the horses other owners contracted her to ride and show. And then what?

Straightening slowly, she hugged her middle. Termination would be the least complicated route, she acknowledged with a heavy heart. But could she do it? She didn't know. Her thoughts were a tangled mess of crushed dreams and a potential career crisis.

But whether or not she had the baby was *her* decision. She had the most to lose either way. As for Xavier…what he didn't know wouldn't hurt him.

Until she made up her mind about her future she couldn't risk him finding out about her condition. She had to get as far away from his influence as possible. But where could she go? Where could she hide?

Before she could flee to lick her wounds and reorganize her life she had to make arrangements for her horses and those she trained for other owners. Because no matter how this ended, she was a professional and she wanted to have a career to return to after…whatever happened.

She pulled out her phone, determined to get business out of the way so she could focus on the multitude of changes ahead. Hannah's number popped up as the missed call. No surprise. Somehow her cousin always knew when Megan needed her, and Hannah would support her no matter which choice she made. Hannah would give her refuge while she tried to make sense of her future.

That took care of the where-to-go problem. It was time to go home to North Carolina—the state and country she'd fled a decade ago—and get as far away from Xavier Alexandre as possible.

Three weeks of silence weighed heavily on Megan's nerves. She hadn't heard from Xavier. He hadn't called, emailed, texted or responded in any way to her email informing him that she wouldn't be returning to France.

She'd expected…something. And yes, it shamed her to admit she'd hoped he'd miss her, come after her, apologize and propose. He was a fighter, not a quitter. His company's rise to the top in the global perfume market proved his ambition and tenacity.

It was hard to accept that the most exciting time of her life, her love affair with the man she'd believed perfect, was over. Finished. And being dismissed so easily hurt in ways she never could have imagined. It was as if she'd never mattered to him and as the cliché said, she was out of sight and out of mind.

But life went on and this morning her cousin Hannah—not Xavier—had accompanied her to her first prenatal appointment—a bittersweet moment filled with both joy and pain.

She'd never planned to have children. But those plans had changed somewhere over the Atlantic when she'd remembered Hannah's mother's favorite saying. *The end of something is always the beginning of something else.*

The words hadn't meant anything to Megan as a child, but they couldn't be more apt now. This baby was the beginning of her new life. And if she couldn't have Xavier, she could have a family of her own.

With her attention only half-focused on the rider in front of her, she thanked heaven for her cousin. Hannah had not only welcomed her and provided her with a home, but she'd helped find experienced riders to keep Megan's horses in shape. And she had made a place for Megan at Sutherland Farm as a trainer and riding coach. It wasn't nearly as satisfying or challenging as riding, but for now, it would pay the bills.

It was only when she wandered through the silent guest cottage—her new home—at night that Megan got caught up in the what-might-have-beens. But she and her baby would survive without Xavier Alexandre.

The sound of a rail clattering down jerked her attention back to the student cantering through the intermediate jump course. Megan signaled the rider—her last lesson of the day—to meet her at the gate. She was used to assessing her competition, analyzing their weaknesses and using those to trounce them in the ring. Finding a constructive way to share a rider's faults and coach them into a better performance wasn't a skill she'd mastered yet. But she was working on it.

"Do you know why that last rail came down, Terri?" she asked as she stroked the big chestnut's glossy neck. The Hanoverian mare had heart and scope. That was half the battle. If only her rider were half as talented.

The girl grimaced. "I rushed it. I was already racing for the time line before I cleared the last vertical."

"Exactly. And your distraction confused your horse. Otherwise, that was a good run. You could lean a little more forward as you approach, but you can work on that between now and your next lesson."

"Got it. I'll see you next week, Megan. Thanks." Terri waved and trotted off on her mare.

Megan's energy flagged. The combination of restless nights combined with her pregnancy was kicking her butt. The course needed resetting for tomorrow's advanced students, but she just couldn't summon any enthusiasm for the task. It would have to wait until morning. Right now she needed a moment to soak up the peace and quiet of the fading day.

She turned her back on the barn and the paperwork waiting on her desk, braced her arms across the top of the white board fence and parked her boot on the bottom rail as she savored the way the setting sun turned the sky sherbet colors as it disappeared behind the tall pines. The sweet aromas of honeysuckle and gardenias permeated the humid air. There was a stillness in the ring just before dusk, a tranquillity that centered the universe on the rider and her mount.

Megan missed riding like an amputee would miss a newly severed limb, and not being able to pit herself and her horse against time and obstacles left her empty and adrift. She'd been a rider since her father had bought her first pony for her fourth birthday. The show ring had been the one place she'd excelled, the only place she'd always fit in, and her last link to her father who'd been a great competitor. But she wouldn't risk hurting her baby—not even for a short ride.

"This is your favorite time of day. Why aren't you riding?"

Xavier.

She startled at the sound of his deep, slightly accented voice, and her boot slipped on the rail, nearly dumping her on her bottom. She quickly regained her balance and spun to face him. Joy, hope and apprehension swirled like a dust devil inside her. He'd come. Finally. The urge to throw herself in his arms bunched inside her like a compacted spring. But she couldn't. Not until she knew his intentions.

The evening breeze tossed his dark hair. His observant green eyes pinned her in place. The shadow of stubble cloaking his jaw, combined with a white silk long-sleeve shirt and black jeans gave him the look of a modern-day pirate. A pirate who had stolen her heart and tossed it overboard like flotsam, she reminded herself.

"What are you doing here?"

"I have come to take you home." His autocratic bearing and commanding tone were so familiar, so dear. She loved his confidence, his swagger. And those were the words she'd been waiting to hear. But...

"You've canceled your wedding?"

His brow creased. "No."

Her balloon of hope deflated. "Are you going to?"

"I cannot."

She'd thought her heart couldn't break any more. Wrong. A fresh stab of pain gouged her. "Then we have nothing more to discuss, Xavier. You're committed to another woman. You've wasted a trip. Climb back in your jet and have a nice flight home. I'll arrange for someone to pack up the rest of my things and get them out of your cottage."

"If you want your belongings come for them yourself."

How like him to be stubborn. "I can't. I have a job here now."

"Teaching riding lessons," he scoffed as if her occupation was no more prestigious than shoveling manure from stalls.

"I like mentoring others." Or she would once she got the hang of it.

"You like teaching. But you *love* riding. Your possessions will be waiting for you when you return. I will not allow anyone else to enter your home."

"Your home. Your name's on the deed."

"That can easily be changed."

"What happens when you marry, Xavier? Do you think your wife will like having your ex-mistress nearby? Or were you expecting us to carry on as lovers after the ceremony?"

"Unlike my mother, I will honor my vows. You may keep the cottage. We are adults. Cecille need not know of our past."

"Everyone knows about us. We were inseparable for months. Ship my stuff here or give it away. I don't care. I'm not coming to get it."

Good thing she'd brought the most important items with her when she'd packed in such a rush to get out before he'd returned from work that day. She wouldn't need the fancy designer dresses he'd bought her since she wouldn't be attending parties with him. Besides, pretty soon they wouldn't fit. She was already noticing her tops fit more snugly.

She wanted to howl in pain and frustration. Couldn't he see he was making a huge mistake? But unless he relented on his marriage plans she couldn't risk returning to the house where she'd been so happy with him—the cottage where she'd finally allowed herself to trust in forever. The memories would undermine her resolve to do the right thing for herself and her baby. Besides, she couldn't afford to have him guess her secret and possibly claim her child.

He moved closer. The fence blocked her retreat. As the distance between them decreased, a slight quiver overtook her body. He lifted a hand and cupped her face in the warmth of his palm. "How can you walk away from what we shared, Megan?"

As tempted as she was to lean into his touch, she resisted. It wasn't easy. "I could ask you the same thing."

"But I am not."

She forced herself to twist out of reach. "Yes, you are. You're engaged to marry someone else. You know I won't settle for second place. I always fight for first—in the ring and out of it. You once told me my zeal was one of the things you liked best about me."

"I admire many things about you, including your ambition and independence. But there is no need to throw a tantrum because you cannot have your way in this."

She gaped at him as anger boiled inside her. "A tantrum! You think I'm throwing a tantrum?"

"What else could it be? I have showered you with gifts. I have even given you a home. I will make sure you lack for nothing even after we end our association. If you return to Grasse."

"I've never cared about your money, your estate, your

fancy cars or airplanes. You're not offering what I want most, Xavier. You. Exclusively."

"You have me exclusively now."

"But only until your wedding. One of these days I'm going to want a husband…and children. I want someone to grow old with. A friend and a lover. You want that with someone else. Do us both a favor and move on."

Her stiff muscles protested as she turned and ordered them to carry her away from the best—*and the worst*—thing that had ever happened to her.

She didn't need to hear gravel crunching under his heels to know Xavier followed. Her body sensed his like a divining rod does water. His purposeful stride quickly brought him up alongside her, and though her eyes hungered for another look at him, she denied herself the pleasure and the pain.

"I have nothing more to say. Goodbye."

"If we are going to quote past conversations, then you will recall that my determination is one of the traits you claimed we shared and you admired. Do not expect me to give up so easily when what we have is so good. I fight for what I want, and I want you, *mon amante*."

"What we *had*. Past tense." Apprehension tightened in her middle. She should have listened to her intuition and refused to ride his horses when he'd first approached her. But she hadn't. She'd been swept away by a man who bought treats for her horses instead of gifts for her, and she'd ignored the warning prickles and signed the contract promising to become his trainer and rider.

After the first competition he'd asked her out while she was still high on the euphoria of winning. She'd somehow found the strength to refuse but then he'd pursued her, unrelentingly bulldozing right over her vow to never become involved with a client.

She couldn't let him overpower her again. She had to get rid of him. But how?

She glared up at him. "Stop following me. I won't play cat and mouse with you. And I won't entertain you until your bride-to-be is willing to warm your sheets. Find another lover, Xavier. I intend to."

A lie. But he didn't need to know that.

The nostrils of his aristocratic nose flared and jealousy ignited in his eyes like twin torches. She only had a moment to enjoy her successful score before he hooked a hand behind her nape, holding her captive as his mouth claimed hers.

Shock stalled her heart before passion spurred it into a galloping beat. It shamed her to admit that even his angry kiss turned her on. But then their sexual compatibility had never been in question.

His lips crushed hers, then softened. He plied her tender flesh with the skill that had slayed her resistance from their first kiss. His tongue traced the seam of her lips. Teasing her. Tempting her. Coaxing a response from her that she didn't want to give.

Oh, yes, she wanted him. Badly. It disgusted her that she could be so easily manipulated. But even her disgust didn't kill the hunger.

One last kiss. And then you say goodbye. And mean it.

She opened her mouth and let him in. His familiar taste overwhelmed her, and she couldn't resist moving closer for a final delicious press of his body against hers. His arms surrounded her, banding her against his muscled length, and his heat seeped into her, warming her for the first time since she'd left him.

She clutched his waist, caressed his strong back. Being with him felt so good, so right. Saying goodbye shouldn't be this hard.

Desire shuddered through her, filling her with a need that only Xavier could satisfy and reminding her how many weeks it had been since she'd shared his body. Love blossomed inside her. How could he not feel it, not want more?

His fingers tightened in her hair. His other hand cupped her bottom, pulling her against the hot, thick column of his erection. He slowly lifted his head. His gaze burned into hers and his breath fanned her skin.

"You are delicious, like the finest wine, the most decadent crème brûlée. I have missed having you in my bed and in my arms, *mon amante*. Come home with me, Megan."

The huskiness of his voice proved he wanted her. Maybe if she reminded him just how good they were together he'd reconsider his disastrous choice and ditch the fiancée.

Risky.

But their passion was the strongest weapon she possessed, and if she could change his mind she'd have everything she never knew she wanted before Xavier—a home of her own, a man who loved her and a family. And her new cottage was conveniently only a few hundred yards away.

"You come home with me." She laced her fingers through his and led him down the driveway. The quarter-mile walk gave the voice in her head plenty of time to insist that this was a foolhardy strategy. But she ignored it.

If she wanted Xavier back, then she had to fight fire with fire.

TWO

Xavier knew he'd won from the moment Megan's lips turned soft and pliable beneath his. He allowed her to take his hand and lead him to her lair. He could afford to be magnanimous in victory.

Seeing the interior of the small stone cottage only confirmed his belief that she had left him to make a point. As charming as her temporary accommodations might be, she had not bothered to make them hers the way she had the house he had provided for her.

If she had intended to stay in the States she would have stamped some trace of her personality in the living area or the bedroom, but the only hint of Megan's occupancy lingered in the air. The bedroom smelled of her and the rose-scented lotion she—or he—smoothed over her skin each night in the ritual he enjoyed watching or sharing. A scent made by one of his low-budget competitors, he recalled with no small amount of distaste.

As good as she smelled, she could smell better if she allowed Parfums Alexandre to blend a personalized fragrance for her. But she had refused his offer.

He surveyed the steep-ceilinged bedroom, taking in the queen-size cherry bed and the traditional, elegant burgundy-and-gold decor. A ceiling fan hanging from one of the exposed crossbeams lazily stirred the air.

The room contained none of the feminine, lacy frills he knew Megan preferred in her linens and in her lingerie. To the world, she was an aggressive competitor and a dedicated horsewoman with a savvy mind for business and an enviable work ethic. He liked knowing that only he saw the soft femininity she concealed beneath her utilitarian riding clothes and no-nonsense attitude.

His heart pounded faster in anticipation of removing her shirt and jeans and uncovering the delicate French undergarments she always wore. He enjoyed buying her sexy lingerie almost as much as he relished removing it and sampling her supple skin.

She stopped beside the bed and tipped her head back to look at him. Her blue eyes were heavy-lidded with desire, her pupils dilated. Her cheeks were flushed and her lips parted. Her hand trembled in his, revealing her eagerness for his caress—an eagerness he shared.

It had been a long, frustrating three weeks waiting for her tantrum to end. It angered him that she had wasted some of the dwindling time they had left. Now that she had come to her senses, they could get on with the pleasure. But he would make her pay for making him come to her. Soon he would have her begging for what she had left behind and their affair would resume. On his terms.

She reached for the buttons of his shirt, releasing them with an enthusiasm that pleased him. Then she unfastened his belt and pants and tugged his shirttail free. A carnal hunger invaded him, making it difficult to force air into his lungs. He reined in the undisciplined feeling.

She parted the fabric of his shirt and cool air swept his chest a split second before her warm hands brushed over him. The need to toss her onto the burgundy-and-gold bedding and sate himself nearly overwhelmed him, but he would let her set the pace. For now. Later, when he had her panting and weak with need he would call the shots.

She bent and touched her lips to his nipple, then flicked the hardened tip with her hot tongue. Desire carved through him like a sharp knife, making him shudder. Only Megan had this incendiary effect on him. He would not give her up. Not yet. Thank God she had moved past her jealous nonsense, and although he did not know what had changed her mind, it did not matter. He had won. As he always did.

Her short nails rasped gently down his sides and then beneath his waistband and around to his fly. She lowered his zipper in slow motion, and he hardened almost to the point of pain. And then she cupped him in her palm. Her touch burned him through his silk boxers and his hips flexed of their own volition as she encircled and stroked him. He clamped his teeth on a moan.

He hooked a hand around her waist, yanked her forward and covered her mouth. She tasted divine, like heady champagne or her favorite Moscato d'Asti. Sweet. Flavorful. Her lips were soft, her tongue slick and hungry as it intertwined with his. His pulse drummed in his ears.

Merde. He could not wait. He hastily unbuttoned and removed her shirt, ripping it down her arms and tossing it aside to reveal a white cotton bra. Surprised, he paused to trace a finger along the plain edge. Her breath caught. "What is this?"

"Um…a sports bra."

He didn't like it. He preferred sheer lace that allowed a

glimpse of her nipples. But on the other hand, this bra made her breasts seem fuller, so perhaps the ugly piece did have some merit. He bent and licked the top of one soft swell and then the other. Her fingers tangled in his hair, holding him close.

Megan had extremely sensitive breasts, and he would use that to his advantage to make her promise to see this affair through until the last possible moment.

He sat on the edge of the bed and pulled her between his legs. Her scent filled his nostrils and her taste tantalized his tongue, urging him to delve into the shadowy cleft. Cupping the pale mounds, he stroked her nipples through the fabric, relishing in the way her flesh sprung to attention beneath his thumbs.

She whimpered. "I've missed this. Missed you, Xavier."

"And I you." He unhooked the unattractive garment and dropped it, eager for more of her skin and a lungful of the headier perfume always lurking between and beneath her breasts, which were definitely rounder, heavier. She must be nearing her monthly cycle. While he feasted on the puckered tips, he used his free hand to flick open her jeans, then pushed them down her legs. He needed to feel her wetness.

He combed his fingers through her tight curls, finding her center. She jerked and gasped. And then he located the prize he sought. She was ready for him. Her hips moved against his hand, encouraging his caress.

His groin pulsed harder, demanding attention. He ached with the need to drive inside her and race toward the release she had denied him for too long. The temptation to do so and take care of her afterward flitted across his mind. But *non.* That was not his way.

Instead he drew a sobering breath and slicked his finger

upward, using her womanly lubricant to tease her while he gently scraped a nipple with his teeth then sucked.

She whimpered his name, clenched her fingers in his hair and bowed her back, offering him a pale feast. A tremor shook her body as he divided his attention between the puckered tips begging for attention. The aroma of her arousal filled the air. He wanted to taste her, but he was precariously close to the edge, and he wanted to make her wait until she was incoherent with need.

Rising, he ripped back the covers, then lifted her into his arms and set her onto the bed. He made quick work of her boots and remaining clothing then his own, pausing only long enough to toss the condom from his pocket on the nightstand.

The sight of her ivory curves spread across the burgundy sheets mesmerized him. Megan possessed an athlete's body, leanly muscled, but softened by her feminine attributes. Her strength was quite a turn-on.

"You are beautiful."

"You make me feel beautiful. Come here." She raised a hand and bent her knee, inviting him into her bed, into her body.

One frayed fiber of self-control remained. He settled on the mattress at her feet and captured a slender arch in his palm. Her eyes widened and her lips parted. She squirmed, knowing what was coming.

Megan's feet, legs and hands were her primary methods of communication with her horses. Over the years, they had become hypersensitive to any nuance. He lifted her foot to his mouth, kissing her big toe, her instep. He rasped his bristly chin on her skin then flicked his tongue over the arch. She shuddered, as he had known she would.

He hid his smile against the tender skin behind her ankle then worked his way up the inside of her calf, pressing her legs apart as he ascended. Megan's fingers fisted in the sheets and her breathing quickened. He savored the satiny skin cloaking firm, tensed muscles and nipped at the soft pad of flesh inside her thighs that she hated. She twisted impatiently. The aroma of her arousal made him dizzy with hunger. He flicked his tongue along the crease of her leg.

She flexed her hips, silently begging him to pleasure her, but he ignored her request—for now—and focused on planting teasing kisses, licks and nips along her bikini line and over her tummy. He swirled his tongue in her navel, and watched goose bumps rise on her skin. Her curls tickled his cheek.

To hell with it. He had hungered for her taste for weeks. He would not deny himself any longer. He cupped her buttocks and flicked her swollen bud with his tongue, slowly at first, then more rapidly. He groaned at the delicious taste of her.

She bucked her hips off the bed. "Oh, Xavier. That feels…so good."

He stroked her in the way he knew would drive her to the edge until her legs quivered. He waited until she hovered on the brink before lifting his head and kissing her thigh. She squeaked a disappointed protest.

"Are you in a hurry, *chérie?*"

"Yes. Yes. It's been so long. I haven't…since you… Please."

That she had not had a release since leaving his bed pleased him inordinately.

"Please what, Megan?" He licked her once, twice, enjoying each flinch and gasp of delight, then stopped again.

She pulled the pillow from beneath her head and whacked him with it. Her playfulness between the sheets was yet another reason he could not let her go. Not yet.

Megan was both his lover and his playmate, and on days when work drove him to the precipice of insanity, she never failed to pull him back and make him smile.

But the desire on her face now, the white teeth digging into her bottom lip, and her passion-filled eyes told the truth. She ached as badly as he and the time for play was over.

"I need you. Now," she pleaded. He liked to hear her beg for him. The growling demand of the last word turned him on.

"Need me how? Like this?" He slid his fingers inside her, drawing out a low, sexy whimper.

"Oh, yes."

"Or this?" He bent to suck her into his mouth while pumping his fingers.

"Yes," she hissed as her orgasm undulated through her.

He rode each jerk of her climax with his hand and mouth, drawing out as much pleasure as he possibly could. The rhythmic clench of her body around his fingers drove him precariously close to losing control. It had been a long time since he had allowed himself release. Doing so without Megan had been less than satisfying and therefore pointless.

The moment her spasms ended, he dove for the condom, rolled it on and hooked his hands behind her knees. "Look at me as I take you, Megan."

Her heavy lids lifted and her dazed eyes met his. "I want you inside me, Xavier. Hurry."

Gritting his teeth against the searing need urging him to race hard and fast to satisfaction, he eased into her slick channel and sank deep into her. The blaze intensified as he withdrew and returned again and again, setting a steady, controlled pace that he hoped would prolong his ecstasy.

But Megan had other ideas. Her hands grasped his

shoulders, pulling his torso closer to hers. Her nails lightly scored trails down his chest, bumping over his nipples and fanning his hunger like bellows. She arched off the bed and planted a wet kiss on his neck, then her tongue outlined the shape of his ear and dipped inside with hot, wet plunges that mirrored his thrusts.

Hunger blasted through him like a furnace. He countered it by focusing on continuing to torment her, but then the pressure swelled inside him and he knew he could not delay any longer.

"Come for me," he ordered, his voice more growl than words as he swiveled his hips against the tender spot that would set her off. Almost instantly her breath caught and her fingers dug into his back. Climax burst through her. The first contraction of her body hit him like a Molotov cocktail. Wave after wave of release reverberated through him until he had nothing left.

No strength in his arms. No air in his lungs. He collapsed to his elbows, momentarily savoring her damp torso against his, then he slowly rolled to her side. The ceiling fan stirred the air, cooling and drying his skin.

No. He would not give up Megan until his vows required they part.

She grabbed his hand, pulled it across her body and rested it on her smooth stomach. He forced his weighted eyelids open and found her eyes on him. Her mouth opened, closed, opened again, but she said nothing.

He understood her speechlessness. His climax had been as stupefying as hers apparently had been. "Come home with me, Megan."

"I'll come as soon as you end your engagement."

His muscles went rigid, his contentment shattered. "I have told you I cannot."

Her face blanched. She threw his hand aside and bolted

upright in the bed. Her eyes turned from soft and sated to wounded and betrayed.

"It will never be this good with *her*."

"I know that, *mon amante*."

Her lips quivered and she nipped the bottom one between her teeth. But she didn't cry. No, his Megan had too much pride for tears—yet another quality he admired about her. She did not indulge in the emotional drama most women employed to get their way.

"Do you really believe you can turn off what we have like a tap? That the feelings will stop just because you order them to?"

He expelled a frustrated breath. Apparently they had not made as much progress as he'd believed. "I assure you it will not be easy. But it must be this way."

She climbed from the bed, stalked across the room and through an open door out of sight. When she returned she had her silk robe wrapped tightly around her. The fire blazing from her eyes had little to do with the passion they had just shared.

"That's where you're wrong. It doesn't have to be this way. I don't have to settle for second. I want more than a temporary affair, Xavier. I *deserve* more. And if that's all you have to offer then I don't need you in my life. Get out and go home."

Another tantrum. How unlike her. Why was she acting so out of character? "As you have said, you will never find passion like ours with anyone else."

She folded her arms across her chest. "Watch me."

Jealousy discharged inside him. She pivoted on her heel and wisely retreated through that same door. The lock clicked, echoing through the silent room.

He heard the shower turn on and cursed. She asked the impossible. He could not break his engagement no matter what games Megan played. Even without the Alexandre estate as incentive, he would not shame his family name the way his father had when he had cast honor aside for "love." The subsequent marriage had failed, and it had cost the Alexandre family everything.

Xavier vaulted off the bed and yanked on his clothing.

He had no intention of repeating his father's mistakes. He would simply find another way to coerce Megan into spending the next eleven months in his bed.

And he'd be damned if he would allow her to take another lover. She belonged to him until he said otherwise.

"You shouldn't be lifting these by yourself. Not in your condition," Hannah chided as she joined Megan in the riding ring.

The diamond engagement ring on her cousin's finger caught the sun and flashed like a strobe light as she grabbed the opposite end of the rail Megan was placing in the cup.

"I'm being careful. And you heard the doctor say I should keep up my regular activities. Except riding. Tim will help me as soon as he finishes cooling down Midnight. He's paying for his lessons by helping me set up the courses three days a week and by exercising my horses."

Hannah set the round pole into position and dusted off her hands. "It's good of you to cut him a deal. You could be teaching only the highest-paying clients. Didn't I predict someone with your qualifications would have your choice of students and a waiting list?"

"You did," Megan conceded. "And thanks for setting that up. I help Tim because he has innate talent and a good horse. He reminds me of me when I first started out on my own—all raw talent and ambition. I'd hate to see him miss the chance to compete because his dad lost his job." She paced off the distance to the next jump.

Hannah accompanied her. "We have a new neighbor."

"Who?"

"No clue. Wyatt said some guy called his office and asked if he knew of any horse farms available in the area." Her cousin's face lit up whenever she mentioned her fiancé and she mentioned him often—in almost every sentence. It was both sweet and a painful reminder of what Megan didn't have.

"Wyatt told him about the property down the road from us being vacant. You probably didn't know ol' Mr. Haithcock died two years ago. His heirs can't come to an agreement over what to do with the property, so it's been sitting vacant. Anyway, Wyatt gave the man the contact information. One of the heirs called to say thanks. The guy leased the farm. That's a load off me because I've been keeping an unofficial eye on the place."

"I drove past the property last week on my way to town. It's in really bad shape." Apprehension prickled Megan's neck. Xavier wouldn't…

Hannah nodded. "Mr. Haithcock's declining health prevented him from keeping up with the maintenance. The fences are falling down, the paint is peeling on all the buildings, the pastures are overgrown and the driveway is so littered with storm debris it looks like an obstacle course. I was considering sending a crew over to mow the fields and clean up a bit just to keep the riffraff and rodents out."

Definitely not Xavier's kind of place. But Megan hadn't heard a word from him in the five days since she'd kicked him out. At the time she'd been too relieved to find him gone when she'd come out of the bathroom to be suspicious. She'd never known him to back down from a challenge.

She put a hand over her belly. "When did all this happen?"

"Hmm. The guy called earlier in the week and Haithcock's

nephew called last night. I've noticed a lot of activity on the farm for the past couple of days, and I passed a horse hauler turning into the driveway on my way home from the wedding planner's just now. I'll say one thing, the new tenants' horses travel first-class. That was an expensive rig."

Panic trickled through Megan. She clutched the oxer's vertical for support. *No. Please no. It's just a coincidence.*

"Megan, are you okay? Did you overdo it? You look like you're about to pass out."

Megan tucked her hair behind her ears with an unsteady hand and forced a smile that almost cracked her face. It couldn't be Xavier. The sprawling cedar ranch home was far too rustic for his caviar tastes, and the barn wasn't nearly as large or posh as his stable. "I'm just borrowing trouble."

"That's not like you. Care to explain?"

Not really. But Hannah could be stubborn. "I had a fleeting thought that Xavier might be laying siege by setting up camp outside the castle walls, so to speak, but I'm sure he's returned to France. After all, I'm not giving him what he wants and he has a wedding to plan and a business to run."

"I hate that I was out when he stopped by. I would have loved to meet him and tell him what a jerk he is."

Megan wasn't surprised by Hannah's protectiveness. She and her cousin had been as close as sisters since the day Megan had moved into the Sutherland house after her family's plane crash. If not for the impossible relationship with Hannah's father nothing could have driven Megan away.

Now that Luthor had retired and moved out, the farm wasn't a battle zone anymore. But the farm was Hannah's and Wyatt's now, and once more, Megan was the outsider looking in. And if Hannah and Wyatt started a family, Megan feared she'd be in the way all over again.

She pushed the unpleasant possibility aside and focused on the more pressing issue. "Hannah, you have no idea how close I came to telling Xavier about the baby. For a few moments after we made love everything seemed so perfect and I felt so close to him. I thought he'd decided to dump his fiancée. I put his hand on my stomach, and I'd taken a breath to share my news. But I just couldn't find the words."

"Good thing you didn't."

"That would have been a disaster."

Hannah pulled her cell phone from her pocket. "I'll call Wyatt and see if Haithcock's heir mentioned the tenant's name."

"That isn't really necessary. I'm sure I'm just being paranoid. This isn't a feudal war, despite Xavier's arranged marriage. Moving horses halfway across the globe in a couple of days and with no prior planning would take an act of Congress. Even if they do have all their paperwork in order."

"We'll both feel better once we're sure." Hannah smiled as she punched in the number. The love and anticipation of talking to her man written all over her face sent a tiny twinge of envy through Megan. Then disappointment replaced Hannah's smile. "It went to voice mail. I forgot he had a conference call this afternoon. I'll ask him tonight."

"It's okay. Really."

But she wouldn't sleep a wink until she knew for sure that Xavier hadn't leased Haithcock's farm. It seemed she would have to drive over to personally welcome the new neighbor.

Megan got a bad feeling as soon as she steered the pickup truck she'd borrowed from Sutherland Farm between the newly repaired and whitewashed fences flanking the Haithcock farm driveway. A fresh layer of gravel crunched beneath her tires.

Then she spotted the top-of-the-line tractor-trailer horse hauler—the kind multimillion-dollar horses rode in. Her stomach sank. This couldn't be good.

She parked beside the luxurious transporter and climbed from the cab. The humid evening air smelled of paint, fresh shavings and recently mowed grass. When she saw the chestnut stallion being led by a groom down the truck's ramp, she broke out in a cold sweat.

She knew that horse as well as she knew her own. His strengths. His weaknesses. His bad habits. His owner.

Xavier.

The urge to bolt for the woods and lose her lunch charged through her, but she gritted her teeth until the nausea passed. Fleeing would be futile anyway. Xavier had already proven he'd follow. With his prize stallion, her favorite mount.

She scanned the now pristine property. How like Xavier to take the old farm from derelict to showplace in just days. He had the means and the money to work miracles.

An odd mixture of hope, dread and excitement fizzed through her. Would he go to so much trouble if he didn't feel something for her? If he didn't want her back? Her and only her. Maybe he'd realized how stupid and anachronistic an arranged marriage was.

The stallion caught her scent. His ears flicked forward and he whickered in recognition. She closed the distance and stroked his glossy neck.

"Hello, Apollo. Where's Mr. Alexandre?" she asked the unfamiliar groom handling the horse.

He pointed toward the freshly painted barn. "Inside."

"Thanks."

Her heart thumped harder as she approached the building. A black Maserati Quattroporte identical to the high-performance luxury sedan Xavier drove at home occupied a spot near the barn's front entrance. She heard his voice before she saw him and then he came through the door with his cell phone to his ear, jolting her to a stomach-dropping halt.

His jade eyes coasted over her, giving her goose bumps. He ended his call. "Good evening, Megan."

She waited for him to tell her he'd made a mistake and wanted her back, but the silence stretched between them. "Why are you doing this, Xavier?"

He shrugged his broad shoulders. "If the rider won't come to the horse, then the horse must come to the rider."

"What happened to the replacement rider I found for him?"

"She was inadequate."

"She's ranked in the top ten."

"Apollo prefers you."

And so do I, she waited for him to add. But he didn't.

"You've put him through a transatlantic flight for nothing. I'm not riding him."

"He and your other mounts will stay until you come to your senses."

Another brick slid down her throat and landed with a *kerthunk* in her belly. "You brought all three of them?"

He inclined his head.

"Why? You're decreasing the value of the animals by pulling them from competition midseason."

"You did that when you abandoned them to a strange and inferior rider. They did not perform as well for her as they did for you."

"You didn't give them a chance to adjust to each other's

styles." But maybe a teensy part of her was happy that the horses had performed better for her. *Petty, Megs.*

"It is done." And once he made a decision, she'd learned, he stuck to it. But she hoped he'd change his mind on one—his marriage.

"How long are you going to play this game, Xavier?"

"I have signed a year's lease."

She smothered a groan. She had to find a way to convince him to go home and soon. She might be able to hide her condition under baggy shirts for another month, but that was it, and in six months she'd have his child. "What about Parfums Alexandre and your upcoming wedding? That's less than a year away?"

"Cecille can plan the nuptials without me, and I will work via conference call for now. And I have the jet on standby."

To him jetting to another country was like any normal person's road trip. Only, he had a full crew so he worked during the flights. "Haithcock's house is hardly up to your five-star standards."

He shrugged. "It has a simple charm and the furnishings provided are adequate."

"You're wasting your time, Xavier."

"You have mentioned competing on the American circuit. I will provide the means for you to do so until you get it out of your system. The horses and you are certainly up to the task. I understand your need to prove your worth although I am told your uncle has retired from the horse business and no longer attends the shows to witness your success."

It shouldn't surprise her that he'd done his homework. "Proving myself on my uncle's turf isn't what this is about."

"Then what is the problem? What keeps you here?"

Had he not heard a word she'd said? *"Her."*

"As I have said before, Cecille is not an issue. I will not leave until you agree to return with me."

"Only one thing will make that happen."

A dark eyebrow lifted.

Her palms turned clammy. "End your engagement."

His expression darkened ominously. "You demand the one concession I cannot grant."

His words punctured whatever remained of her balloon of hope. If he loved her he wouldn't hurt her this way. No, they'd never spoken the words, but the closeness they'd shared, the amount of time they'd spent together, had led her to believe he cared. He allowed her to see a side of himself that others never saw—a side that was gentle instead of ruthless, considerate instead of conquering. Had that meant nothing to him at all?

"How does your fiancée feel about your extended vacation?"

"I did not ask her opinion."

She gaped at him. Was he clueless? "I realize you didn't have a good role model, so let me help you. Marriage is a partnership. It means always considering the feelings of your significant other before making decisions that will affect him or her. Cheating on your future wife with a mistress—even if that mistress is across an ocean—is hardly the way to earn trust and make a relationship last."

"And you are an expert on long-term relationships? I think not. The only lasting associations you have had are with your cousin and your horses. You thrive on competition, Megan. Why are you not competing?"

She scrambled for an acceptable response. One he'd believe. One that would convince him he couldn't change her mind. Unless he changed his first.

"I've chased the dream of being on top of the leaderboard for ten years. I'm tired and need a break. I miss my cousin.

I want to help Hannah plan her wedding. And now that my uncle has moved away from Sutherland Farm, there's no reason for me to avoid the place. I'm leaving the European Circuit for good, Xavier. I won't come back. Not for you or your horses. Not if you're married to *her*."

The minute she said the words she knew they were true. She couldn't go back if he married that woman. Megan couldn't bear to see Xavier and his wife in the stands or at the pre- and post-show parties. They'd bump into each other constantly. And knowing Xavier's have-his-cake-and-eat-it-too attitude, he'd probably expect her to keep riding his horses even after he said his vows.

The life she'd built in Europe was over and the friends she'd made relegated to the past. The realization hit hard, and even though she'd left a month ago a part of her had hoped to return. But that wasn't looking likely. Her emotions, which had been close to the surface lately, threatened to mutiny. Her eyes and throat burned and her chest tightened.

She would not cry. Especially not in front of Xavier. Gritting her teeth and fighting for composure, she turned on her heel and stalked away. She kept her eyes focused on the truck and escape.

"Why are you trying to change the rules of our affair?" he called after her.

Amazed that such a brilliant man could be so obtuse, she stopped and pivoted. "For the past six months we have spent nearly every hour together when we're not working. I thought the rules had already changed."

"Non."

"Do you love me, Xavier?"

Rejection stamped his face. "Love was never part of our agreement."

"Our agreement? You make our relationship sound like a business deal sealed with a handshake."

"Are you claiming you love me?" He didn't sound as though the idea appealed, and the fact that he avoided answering her question was answer enough.

Disillusionment settled heavily on her shoulders. "I believed I did. But I guess I was mistaken. You aren't the man I thought you were, because that man would never subject his wife and his children or his lover to the humiliation of the gossip we both know runs rampant on the circuit.

"You may not care about the whispers that will go on behind your future wife's back or mine, but I do, Xavier, and I won't embarrass her or cheapen myself. I'm going to say it one last time. Maybe this time you'll hear me. Go home. As long as you're planning to marry her, there's nothing for you here."

Three

Megan stared at the fuzzy white image on the screen, too choked up to speak. That beating heart, those little hands and feet, tiny fingers and toes, eyes and mouth belonged to her baby. Hers and Xavier's.

As if sensing the emotion damming Megan's throat, Hannah squeezed her hand.

The obstetrician pushed a button on the ultrasound machine and the printer started humming. She wiped the gel from Megan's stomach and helped her sit up. "Megan, everything looks exactly as it should for twelve weeks gestation. I'd guestimate your due date is the first week of January. You should have a new baby to start the New Year."

A new year. A new life. Alone with her baby. She'd better get used to doing things without Xavier.

"Can you tell if it's a girl or boy yet?" Hannah asked the doctor, making Megan glad she'd brought her cousin along for moral support since her brain refused to produce the appropriate questions.

"Not yet. But since we're unclear on the date of your last period we'll repeat the ultrasound in eight weeks just to confirm our dates. We might get a better picture then. Any more questions?"

When Megan shook her head, the doctor handed her the printed picture, wished her well and left the small room. Megan stared at the image, a tangle of emotions weaving through her. Excitement. Happiness. Sadness. Fear. She would be responsible for this little person, for his or her health and happiness and well-being. Her and her alone. What if she messed up?

"You okay?" Hannah asked.

Megan slid off the table and straightened her clothes. "Xavier should have been here for this."

"It's his loss, Megs."

What if one parent wasn't enough? What if something happened to her? Who would care for her baby? "Maybe I should tell him."

"Do you think telling him would make him dump her and marry you?"

"That's the million-dollar question—one I've asked myself a zillion times. I don't know. On one hand, once Xavier sets a course he never deviates. On the other, what's his is his. He doesn't give up easily."

"If you told him and he dumped her and married you would you always wonder if he'd done so just because of the baby?"

Leave it to Hannah to get to the heart of the matter. "Yes. I want him to wake up and realize that what we have—what I thought we had—is too special to throw away."

"Then postpone telling him a little longer. If he hangs

around you'll have no choice. But for now wait and see if he comes to his senses."

"Right. For now I'll carry on." Alone. The way she always had since her parents' and brother's deaths.

After his confrontation with Megan three days ago, Xavier had been ready to say to hell with her, fly himself and his horses back to France and let her suffer for her foolishness. Replacing her would be easy enough.

But he didn't want any other woman.

He craved Megan. She was in his blood like a narcotic. He had to make her understand that what they had— combustible sex, mutual respect and similar interests— had nothing to do with his marriage. That alliance was business, whereas they shared pure pleasure. And he wanted to drink in as much of that pleasure as he could. After his marriage he would have to suffice with duty, honor and obligation. Not that Cecille was unattractive. But she was not Megan.

If he could not get what he wanted from Megan directly, he would have to use alternative means. Targeting Wyatt Jacobs, the CEO of Triple Crown Distillery and co-owner of Sutherland Farm where Megan resided, was the only strategy Xavier could think of for getting closer to Megan. He needed to know whether her abrupt departure was simply jealousy or something more. He was beginning to suspect the latter.

She had always been strong, determined and logical. He admired that about her. But she had an inflexibility to her attitude now, and her decision to abandon the career she loved was most definitely illogical and therefore out of character.

He shook Wyatt Jacobs's hand. "Thank you for helping me find the farm and agreeing to see me."

"Your offer to give me the inside track on corporate sponsorship of Grand Prix events is hard to refuse. It's something I've been considering for a while but other priorities have prevented me from doing the required research."

"My sources told me that your company was preparing to launch a high-end whiskey. I have never seen your brand connected with equestrian events. It is a missed opportunity—especially given your new ties to Sutherland Farm."

"True. The advertising information you sent me is timely." Jacobs led Xavier through the foyer and into his study and gestured toward a leather visitor chair. He settled behind his desk. "Now that I've begun watching Grand Prix events on TV with my fiancée, I appreciate Parfums Alexandre's visible presence."

"As you can see from the numbers, we have had a good return on our investments. Our ads reach a target market that can afford our product. You could do the same."

"I see your point. Grand Prix attendees are the right demographic. I also want to surprise Hannah by helping her horse rescue operation. The best way to do that is through public awareness—an area in which you have expertise. I won't mention this to her until it's a done deal, so please keep that information to yourself."

"Certainly." Xavier was glad he had educated himself on Hannah Sutherland's horse rescue operation and therapeutic riding program. "Find Your Center is a worthy cause. The equestrian audience should be both sympathetic and generous."

Jacobs sat back in his chair, his eyes shrewd and assessing. "What do you want in return for sharing your knowledge?"

Xavier appreciated a man who was smart enough to

know nothing came freely and one who got to the point. "~
have relocated three of my horses to the Haithcock farm
I need expert riders to exercise and show them, but I hav◄
few connections in the States."

"That would be Hannah's area of expertise, but since ~
doubt she's going to volunteer information, I'll introduc◄
you to the stable's office staff and instruct them to assis◄
you."

"I would prefer to have Megan back."

"Ah. The real reason for your visit. Megan doesn't worl◄
for me. I can't order her to ride for you. You'll have t◄
convince her."

He bit back his frustration. "I understand."

While he listened to his host, Xavier kept an ear ope◄
for signs of Megan's presence—her voice, her step, he◄
laughter—since one of the barn staff had told him she wa◄
with her cousin. But he had yet to see or hear her in th◄
house. He heard steps in the hall and straightened.

"If you're listening for Megan she's not here. That's wh◄
I agreed to meet you today. She and Hannah have gon◄
into town to run some errands—probably a good thin◄
since you're not on either lady's list of favorite people a◄
the moment. I'll probably catch hell for helping you. Bu◄
their feelings are personal and our discussion is business.◄

The weight settling on Xavier's chest was not dis◄
appointment. He was not mooning after Megan like ◄
schoolboy. "I agree. Megan and I—"

Wyatt held up a hand. "What's between you and Mega◄
is none of my concern as long as it's not illegal."

"No. It is not."

Jacobs rose and crossed to a bar. "Would you care t◄
sample Triple Crown's new product? My stepfather starte◄
the process for this single malt before his Alzheimer'◄

became an issue. Launching it successfully while he's still aware of the process is the least I can do for him."

If sharing a drink would ensure Jacobs's cooperation, Xavier would willingly swill pond scum. "Certainly."

His host splashed mahogany liquid into two tumblers. Xavier accepted one. *"Salut."*

He sipped, letting the aged whiskey roll around on his tongue. Nice. Definitely not pond scum. "Very smooth with hints of smoke, caramel and chocolate."

"You have an experienced palate and a good head for business. But let me warn you, Mr. Alexandre. Hurting Megan hurts Hannah. And I won't tolerate anyone hurting my fiancée."

Xavier accepted the warning with a nod. "Understood."

He had an ally—albeit a cautious one.

Megan's heart balked when she spotted the tall silhouette against the white rails. She'd recognize those broad shoulders anywhere. "Stop the car."

Hannah braked without hesitation. "Why?"

"Xavier's here." Megan nodded toward the man by the riding ring.

"I'll call security and have him thrown off the property."

A horse and rider came into view, sailing over the hog's-back jump she'd set up for this afternoon's advanced student. "Wait. That's Apollo. With Tim in the saddle."

"The stallion you used to ride for Xavier?"

"Yes. What is Xavier up to now?"

"Trying to get your attention would be my guess."

"Well, tough. I'm not up for another confrontation. Could you drop me off at the cottage?"

"I'll do that after we find out who gave that jerk permission to be here. Somebody must have. My guess is

Wyatt. I knew not telling him about your pregnancy was a mistake." Hannah put the car into motion and did a U-turn.

"The fewer people who know, the better my chances are of keeping Xavier from finding out before he loses interest in the chase and returns to France."

"If he stays he'll find out anyway."

"I know, but I'm willing to bet he'll leave as soon as I convince him I'm not going to follow him home like a lost puppy."

They parked by the big house. Megan climbed from the car and trailed Hannah to the study where Wyatt sat behind his big desk. It felt so different to come here now when she didn't have to tippy-toe to avoid yet another reprimand from Hannah's father.

Wyatt rose immediately and crossed the room to greet Hannah with a hug and a kiss. Megan averted her face to the tender moment. After this morning's realization that she'd better get used to doing things on her own, their obvious love for each other was more than she could handle.

"Did you know Xavier Alexandre is at the stables?" Hannah asked.

"Yes. I've given him permission to interview our riders."

Dread filled Megan. She couldn't risk bumping into Xavier at every turn.

"You've what?" Hannah practically screeched, extracting herself from her fiancé's embrace.

"Xavier is giving me inside information on advertising on the Grand Prix circuit for the new product launch. In return I'm granting him access to our riders so he can select one or more to exhibit his horses. He said Megan refused."

"Of course she did."

"Hannah, baby, this is business. Your feud is personal."

"But how can you let him on this property after the way he's treated Megan?"

Megan winced. She didn't want to be the cause of contention between the lovebirds. "Hey, guys, no need to fight."

"Relationships end." Wyatt's brown eyes turned to Megan. "Can't you and he handle this situation like adults?"

Megan's mouth opened, closed. Her tongue felt as dry as an old sock. "It's a little more complicated than that."

"Did he ever hurt you? By that I mean physically abuse you or threaten to do so?"

"No."

"Is he threatening you now?"

She exhaled slowly, resignation settling like a lead weight on her shoulders. Apparently the men were going to side together. "No."

"Wyatt, that's not the point. She's pregnant and he can't find out."

"Hannah!" Megan squeaked in dismay.

Her cousin grimaced. "I'm sorry, Megan, but Wyatt needs to understand why you've refused to ride Xavier's horses and why we can't allow him on our property."

Again Wyatt's gaze drilled Megan's, making her yearn for the solitude of her cottage. "The baby's his?"

"Yes."

"You haven't told him?"

"No. Given the fact that he's engaged to someone else, I didn't want to risk a custody battle—one I can't afford and might lose."

Wyatt's face softened only slightly. "Megan, the man has a right to know he's going to be a father. I'd want to know."

Hannah made a disgusted sound. "Leave it to a man to take the two-timer's side."

"I'm not condoning his actions, but he has financial obligations to Megan and their child."

"No." The word burst from Megan. She grappled for a way to make him understand. "Wyatt, I know you mean well, but you have no idea how it feels to be raised by someone out of duty, to always know you are an unwanted burden. I do. Xavier has made it clear that he doesn't want children with me. And I don't want my baby to ever feel unwanted or in the way. I will manage without Xavier's help—financial or otherwise."

Wyatt searched her face and then Hannah's. Something he saw in her cousin's expression made his lips flatten, but the resolution in his eyes didn't bode well for Megan. "He needs to be told."

Not what she wanted to hear. "You don't understand. Xavier never loses."

"Would you rather live your life in fear of him discovering you've kept his child from him? You'll always be looking over your shoulder and waiting to get caught—especially if you stay in the horse business. You can't run from this, Megan. It's a fight you're going to have to face, and it's best to do so on your terms. I'll help you find the best international custody lawyer available."

Hannah grimaced and threw an arm around Megan's shoulders. "Unfortunately Wyatt's right."

"That's not what you said an hour ago," Megan protested.

"An hour ago, I hadn't considered it from this perspective. If you go back on the circuit, someone is going to see your baby and put the pieces together. Even if you don't go back to riding, Sutherland Farm has a global client list. By then, Xavier might be married and have more children with his wife. It's best to tell him the truth now and get this dealt with before he finds out on his own."

Megan's stomach turned queasy, making her regret the

grilled bacon-and-cheese sandwich she'd had for lunch. She'd lost her allies. And, if she wasn't careful, she could lose her baby.

Xavier knocked on Megan's door for the second time. He scanned the surrounding yard when she did not answer. He knew she was here. He had seen her return from her morning run from the vantage point of Wyatt Jacobs's patio.

He checked his watch. Less than ten minutes had passed since she had entered the cottage. It had taken him that long to conclude his follow-up meeting with Jacobs and drive the short distance to Megan's temporary accommodations.

Irritation crawled across his skin. Was she avoiding him? It was not like her to be so childish, but she had been acting strangely since the news of his engagement had surfaced. Cecille should have warned him that she had released the announcement. Then he could have prepared Megan.

The fallout had taught him one thing: Megan loved him. She might deny it now, but he did not believe her. And while he hated that they would inevitably have to part, that had been the plan all along. There was no reason they could not enjoy the next eleven months. Eleven *short* months. Remorse settled heavily in his chest, but he kicked it aside. The arrangements had been made and he would follow through.

Tired of waiting, he grasped the knob and gave it a twist. As he expected, Megan hadn't bothered to lock her door. The woman was entirely too trusting. He pushed his way in, ears attuned, eyes scanning. The sound of splashing water caught his attention and revealed the reason she had not responded to his knock. He should have remembered Megan always showered after her run. She would not have heard his summons over the water.

A mental image of her naked, wet body, her ivory skin and subtle curves accelerated his pulse and spiked a ferocious hunger within him.

Too bad his course had been set years before they had met. But still, he could give Megan the world. Anything her heart desired. Except marriage. Children. And love. He never intended to enter that delusional state. Love made a man forget the things that mattered, like honor and obligations.

He would take advantage of her absence to set up his surprise. He located the kitchen and set the pastry box on the table, then he quietly searched the cabinets until he found plates and set the table. The cold, empty coffeepot took him aback. To Megan, morning coffee was a sacred experience. Watching her sip from her mug, roll the liquid around on her tongue, then swallow with an expression of pure bliss had always been excruciatingly arousing. She'd often worn the same expression when she had traced her tongue around his—

He severed the torturous thought and turned to locate filters and grounds—not her usual gourmet brand—then started a pot in the inferior drip-type machine Americans preferred. She would want the beverage to go with the *croissant amande* he had had flown in fresh this morning from her favorite *patisserie*.

Until she agreed to return home with him, he would remind her at every turn of the life she had left behind—the life she could have again if she would give up her stubborn insistence on exceeding their original agreement.

Once he had plated the pastries to his satisfaction he chose a chair at the table that allowed him a clear view down the short hall to the open bathroom door. Steam rolled into the hallway, carrying the familiar scent of her shampoo. The eagerness to see her, taste her, to thrust inside her again ambushed him. The urge to join her in the shower almost overwhelmed him. Back home he would have.

He would have stripped off his clothing, climbed into the shower stall and smoothed his hands over her wet breasts, her tight nipples then delved into the folds concealed by her curls, arousing her until she begged for mercy. Only then would he have planted her hands against the tile wall and taken her from behind, riding her like a stallion rides a mare.

Sweat beaded on his skin and his pulse raced. His trousers grew tight. He blew out a steadying breath and checked his watch again, his patience wearing thin. She was taking longer than usual in the shower. And then it registered that she wasn't humming. Megan always hummed in the shower. Unless he was with her. Then she moaned. He made sure of it.

Desire pulsed through him. He shifted in his seat, seeking a more comfortable position but not finding one in the antique chair. The water shut off. His muscles tensed in anticipation.

Her arm reached out, snagged a towel then retreated like a striptease to whet his appetite. A long, sleek leg appeared, followed by the rest of her glistening body. She had her back to him. Even from this distance he could make out the droplets snaking down her spine and over her round bottom—a trail he yearned to follow with his tongue. His heartbeat drummed in his ears when she lifted her arms to dry her hair, her face. Megan was an athlete, as her firm, smooth muscles attested, but she was also all woman.

He resented the hell out of the fact that he couldn't see the dusky tips of her breasts as she blotted them dry. She sawed the towel back and forth from her shoulders to her waist and over her delicious *derrière*. Then she leaned over to wipe the moisture from her sleek legs. He nearly groaned at the inviting sight of her moist, pink center.

He wanted to demand she turn, but preferred not to interrupt the seductive show. Had her nipples puckered in the cool air? Had she trimmed the dark triangle of curls during her shower as she sometimes did or left them natural as they had been the other day? Either way he yearned to touch, to taste, to immerse himself in her womanly aroma.

She pivoted slowly to face the mirror with the towel bunched at her middle, giving him a delicious silhouette of her breasts, her buttocks and her long legs—legs that were sleekly muscled from riding her horses. From riding him. His fingertips dug into the arms of the wooden chair—a poor substitute for her satiny skin and supple sinew.

She dropped the towel on the counter and cupped her breasts as if weighing them, her thumbs flicking across her nipples. His pulse raced faster at the sensual gesture. He experienced only a slight twinge of guilt over his enjoyment at his voyeuristic behavior. Then her hands stroked downward, but instead of venturing into her curls and pleasuring herself as he'd expected, her fingers stopped at her waist and splayed over her stomach.

The universal gesture of a mother and her unborn child.

Denial screamed through him. Megan could not be pregnant.

Yes, she had perhaps gained weight, but that was the only reason her breasts were fuller and her stomach slightly rounded.

But she wasn't riding or drinking coffee. And she'd left him after speaking some nonsense about wanting children.

When he put the clues together, he didn't like the inescapable conclusion.

His heart slammed against his rib cage. *No!*

As if suddenly sensing his dismay, she turned abruptly.

Horror widened her eyes and parted her lips. She snatched up the towel, clutching it in front of her like a shield and backing a step.

"What are you doing in my house? You have no right to be here. Get out."

"You're pregnant."

She gasped and paled.

"That is why you left me and why you are not riding." He rose on legs as weak and unsteady as a newborn colt's. Fury and jealously vied for supremacy inside him. "Whose is it? It can't be mine. We used protection. Every time."

"You're right. We used protection. Every time." She parroted back in monotone, then ducked behind the door only to reappear wearing her robe belted tightly around her middle. A middle that nurtured another man's baby.

Damn her. Damn her to hell.

He couldn't believe she would take a lover—not after the passion they had shared, after the way he had pampered her. Not after all her claims of loving him.

Yet the evidence spoke to the contrary, did it not? Anger and resentment burned like acid in his belly and up his throat.

"Whose is it?" he repeated.

"I can't believe you have the audacity to ask that."

"When did you have time to rendezvous with someone else? You were with your horses every day, and we were together every night."

"Does it matter?"

Megan preferred honesty to evasion—no matter how difficult the revelation might be to hear. Her refusal to give a straight answer now said more than words. Who was she protecting?

"You betrayed me," he growled through the rage constricting his throat.

Fury lit her eyes. She charged into the kitchen. "*I'm* the one who was betrayed, Xavier. Not you. The entire time you were making love to me, you were planning to marry someone else, and you didn't even have the decency to tell me."

Remorse needled his skin. He rammed it aside. He had no reason to feel shame. "I was frank about my intentions from the beginning. You are the one who did not abide by our agreement—a temporary, *exclusive* affair with no strings or complications." He pointed at her belly. "This is a complication."

She shifted uneasily then shuffled toward the refrigerator, but made no effort to take anything out of it. Her behavior struck him as odd. Then he vaguely recalled a fuzzy black-and-white image taped to the door that he'd ignored earlier when he had retrieved the skim milk. He gripped her shoulders and moved her out of the way.

"Hey. You can't—" She slapped a hand out, but not before he snatched the print. "Give me that, Xavier."

He studied the shape. He'd seen ultrasound images before—mostly of horse fetuses, but also a few belonging to friends gushing about their imminent parenthood. "This is your baby."

She swiped at it again, but he held it out of reach. "Yes. Give me the picture."

And then the black writing stamped in the white border registered. Today's date and the words *12 Weeks*.

"You're three months pregnant." His mind spiraled back.

"So?" she snipped, folding her arms and lifting her chin.

But it was the fear lurking in her eyes, rather than her defiant posture, that caught his attention. He had never given Megan cause to fear him, and there could only be one reason she would do so now.

A deadly calm settled over him, clarifying his thoughts.

If the child were someone else's, she would have no reason for trepidation. "You love me. You would not have been intimate with another man."

Resignation slowly crept across her features and her shoulders slumped. "No, I wouldn't have cheated."

"The child is mine."

"Not if you don't want it to be."

"What does that mean?"

"It means, Xavier, you can walk out that door right now and never look back. Forget we ever had this conversation and go on with your life, your marriage."

Again, not the answer he had expected. "Did you arrange this 'accident' to coerce me into marrying you?"

She scowled. "If I had, don't you think I would have told you? What good is leverage if you don't use it?"

"Perhaps you intended to wait until after the *bébé* was born to make a claim and the engagement announcement foiled your plan."

"Do you really believe I'd do that to you? Do you trust me so little?"

As far as he knew, Megan had never lied to him. "How—When did this happen?"

She sighed and pushed a tangled lock of damp hair from her face. "I don't know. I'm guessing Madrid. Remember when we ran out of condoms, and you bought some from that sketchy little shop near the show grounds? Maybe then."

His body throbbed at the memory. "We ran out of protection because you were insatiable."

Her face flushed. "Winning does that to me, and that was a really good weekend for me and my horses. You should know. You collected a ton of prize money. But you were the one who couldn't wait until we returned to the hotel."

So he had been. Recalling that lust-filled afternoon made his body overheat. He had nearly taken her in the dark corner of the *petit magasin* where they had purchased the dusty box of condoms. As it was, he had barely been able to restrain himself until he could drag her into the dressing rooms of the show grounds for hard, fast, as-silent-as-they-could-make-it sex.

All that was irrelevant now. "How long have you known?"

She clutched the collar of her robe so tightly her knuckles blanched. "I found out about an hour before I learned of your engagement."

Which explained the unpleasant scene in her cottage and her abrupt departure. "Why did you not inform me then?"

"Because you said you didn't want children with me. That our relationship was *casual*."

"That was our agreement."

"We also agreed that either of us could end it at any time with no hard feelings. Well, I ended it. You're the one who screwed up everything by following me here. But you can go home to your future wife. She'll provide you with heirs and I—" Her voice broke. She pressed her lips together and closed her eyes as if struggling for composure. "I'll have my baby. We'll be fine without you."

He battled the frustration boiling inside him. After more than a decade of plotting, he was on the verge of regaining his ancestral lands and restoring the pride his father had carelessly stripped from the Alexandre name.

Megan's pregnancy jeopardized everything. She carried his child, putting him in the same foolish and precarious position his father had been in thirty-five years ago.

Xavier could blame no one but himself for repeating his father's mistake of impregnating the wrong woman. But he would not replicate the mistakes his father had made afterward by abandoning his bride-to-be at the altar and destroying the strong business alliance his marriage would forge.

But he, unlike his mother, could never abandon his child.

He stared at the small, blurry image in the photograph, barely discernable as human. Arms, legs, hands, fingers, toes. His child. His son or daughter. His heir. The weight of generations of Alexandres settled on his shoulders.

He had to find a solution to this dilemma or this *bébé* could cost him everything.

Four

"How could you not have known about your condition sooner? When we could have dealt with this appropriately?"

Xavier's angry questions hit Megan like a sharp kick. His meaning couldn't be clearer. He would have asked her to terminate the pregnancy.

"*Appropriately* meaning you would have pressured me to get rid of it."

"I did not say that."

"But that's what you meant. You don't want *me* having your child." The realization shattered what was left of her dream that he might suddenly declare his love, marry her and raise a family with her. Not just because of the baby, but because he loved her and couldn't live without her.

"The *bébé* is a complication."

His words landed another blow. Hugging her middle did nothing to soothe the bone-deep pain radiating through her.

"Answer my question, Megan. How could you not have suspected something was amiss sooner?"

"I've never been regular. And when I'm under a lot of pressure, I sometimes skip—" She bit her tongue, damming the words. It didn't feel right to discuss such personal issues with him. Not anymore.

"Did you not give a thought to what this will do to your career? How damaging it will be to your ranking and your business to take time off?"

"I've thought of little else. But I can live with the consequences."

"Your focus and your determination to accomplish your goals—traits I thought we shared—are what I admired most about you. And now you are willing to walk away from years of sacrifice for an unplanned baby?"

Unable to look at his condemnation, she averted her eyes. Her gaze landed on the full pot of coffee, and suddenly the aroma of the fresh brew penetrated her misery. Then the rest of her senses clamored to life. Did she smell butter and almonds?

She scanned the kitchen and spotted a platter in the center of her table piled high with flaky golden pastries. Her mouth watered. "What's that?"

But she—and every one of her taste buds—knew the answer.

Xavier glanced over his shoulder, as if he'd forgotten the delicacies he'd piled on the table behind him. "I had your favorite pastries flown in. You always claimed you would expire without your *croissant amande* fix."

Megan bit her lip and pressed a hand to the ache in her chest. Ridiculously over-the-top romantic gestures like this were only one of the reasons she'd fallen in love with him. "I was exaggerating. Slightly."

As bizarre as it seemed, though her heart was breaking,

her stomach demanded attention. It growled audibly, assuring her she could easily devour the mountain of croissants in one sitting. She had never experienced that kind of appetite in her prepregnancy life, but in the past couple of weeks she'd eaten like a three-hundred-pound football player. If Xavier ever saw her eat like that he'd be appalled.

She had to get rid of him before she made a pig of herself. "Xavier, it's very thoughtful of you to go to all this trouble, but I'm going to have to ask you to leave. I have to get ready for work."

He made no move toward the door. Instead his brow furrowed. "I will raise the child."

She recoiled. *"No!"*

"Doing so will permit you to return to competition."

"If—when—the time is right, I'll go back on the circuit."

"Will you be able to afford a nanny?"

"I'll find a way to make it work."

"I will give you a million dollars for the child."

Shock stole her breath. "This isn't about money, Xavier. I have never wanted your money."

"Then consider the child. I can provide more stability for it than your vagabond life on the road."

But it wouldn't be a life filled with the love and laughter and joy Megan had shared with her parents and brother. They'd been a team, a cohesive unit—her mother and brother and her on the sidelines cheering her father on until her family had died and left her behind. She should have been on that plane with them—would have been aboard if she hadn't been at home with chicken pox.

"Your wife might object to you bringing home a baby."

"Cecille will do as I say."

One of these days his entitled attitude and assumption that everyone would happily jump to do his bidding was going to slap him with a dose of reality. Perhaps she'd had a lucky escape. Too bad her heart refused to believe it.

"Your marriage is doomed to fail with that mind-set."

"I do not fail."

No. He didn't. And that worried her. If this turned into a custody battle her chances of winning were slim even with Wyatt's promise of a great lawyer.

"Xavier, I have never asked you for anything. But I'm asking now. Please forget all about me. About us." She rested her hand on her stomach. "Go home to your fiancée, get married and have your perfect family. And forget you ever knew me."

His eyebrows slammed down. "*C'est impossible.* You are carrying my heir. I will leave you to reflect on my offer. You will see that it is best for the child to reside with me."

Megan wouldn't let Xavier's gifts weaken her resolve to do the right thing for her baby.

She set the platter of croissants on the table in the stable's empty break room for the staff to enjoy, but her fingers refused to heed her brain's command to release the dish.

Her willpower wavered. Maybe she could have just one flaky, crispy, sweet, buttery—

"Should I schedule an intervention?" Hannah asked from behind her.

Megan jumped and snatched her hands away. "Oh. No. I'm— I thought I'd—" She sighed. "Yes. Someone needs to take these away before I give in to temptation and eat the whole batch."

"Are those the famous almond croissants you've raved about for the past year?"

Megan nodded.

"How many have you already eaten?"

"None. Yet. I'm resisting. But it isn't easy." A crumb

clung to her fingertip. Her mouth salivated in anticipation and her arm lifted a few inches before she fought off the urge to lap up the tiny morsel. She dusted off her hands and backed another step away from the tempting confections. "Xavier had them flown in fresh this morning."

"Nice of him. So why are you torturing yourself? It's not as if you need to diet."

Megan shrugged, aiming for a casual dismissal to keep her cousin from worrying. Hannah was head-over-heels in love and about to marry the man of her dreams. The last thing Megan wanted was to bring her off that natural high. "They were a bribe to convince me to continue being his mistress until his wedding."

"Until his— What an egotistical, selfish jerk."

So much for not upsetting the bride-to-be. Hannah looked angry enough to wring Xavier's neck should he be unfortunate enough to stroll in. "That's the least of my problems now. Hannah, he knows about the baby."

Surprise rounded Hannah's eyes and mouth. "You told him?"

"No, he walked in on me this morning when I was getting out of the shower and…"

"And…? Don't leave me hanging."

"He accused me of having an affair."

"The bastard—"

"Then he realized I wouldn't cheat on him and said he wants his child. But not me." Swallowing razor blades would have hurt less than saying the words.

"Oh, Megan, I'm sorry."

"He offered to buy the baby."

"*Sonofabi*—" Hannah bit off the curse and looked over her shoulder as if checking to see if any of the young riders were present. She looked livid, her face red and her fists clenched. "What are you going to do?"

"I'm not selling my baby, and I'm not going to be his mistress until the wedding, that's for sure. But beyond that I don't know. I guess I have to wait for his next move."

"It's not like you to take a wait-and-see attitude. Let me play devil's advocate. Do you still love him? Although I don't know why you would after this. What a creep."

Megan had to bite her tongue to keep from springing to Xavier's defense. He was being a creep right now. But leave it to logical Hannah to get straight to the point. Again.

Aggravated with herself for not being able to crush her feelings for Xavier, Megan stubbed the toe of her boot into the tile floor. "Yes, I still love him. But I'll get over that. Won't I? I mean, how could I not with the idiotic way he's acting?"

Hannah's expression turned sympathetic. "I wish I could guarantee that. But I can't."

"What's wrong with me? I shouldn't have any trouble saying goodbye and good riddance to someone who wants to buy my baby like a black market special and use me to cheat on his fiancée."

Hannah crossed the room and wrapped an arm around Megan's shoulders. "Megan, you are the most proactive and competitive person I know. You're constantly thinking ahead and you never quit when you want something. Your ability to assess your opponent's weaknesses and use them to defeat him is a skill I have always envied. And yet this time, you're surrendering without a fight. Why is that?"

"I'm not surrendering!"

"I mean you're not going after Xavier with anything near the ferocity you'd show to the rider ahead of you on the leaderboard. Why is that?"

Hannah's statement sobered Megan as effectively as a dunk in an icy pond. Why *wasn't* she fighting harder? Other than her initial bid to seduce Xavier into acknowledging their magic, she hadn't tried to plot an alternative strategy. She always had a plan A, plan B and, when necessary, a plan C.

"I guess competing on the Grand Prix circuit was never this…personal. There are always other horse shows and other chances for blue ribbons and prize purses. But this is my baby. Maybe the only shot at motherhood I'll ever have."

"You don't know that. You're only twenty-eight."

"I never planned to have children. Not with my career. And I've never been in love before. Not even close. I can't believe I let myself fall for him. It's not like I wasn't warned that he never stayed long with any lover. He had a reputation as a ladies' man before I met him. But when he was with me he never looked at another woman. And he made me feel…special." She sighed and shoved a hand through her hair. "I thought we were perfect together."

"What makes you so sure you're not? I've never heard you happier than when you talked about him. Don't get me wrong. The man needs a serious attitude adjustment. But if he's truly the only one you want then remember he came all the way across the Atlantic for you."

Megan waved that observation aside. "He has a private jet and a pilot at his disposal, so zipping from one continent to another is no big deal for him."

"But, Megs, he's still here with his horses, and he's paid a year's lease on a farm that you said was far below his standards."

She tried to squash the hope sparking inside her. "He's wealthy enough he'd never miss the money if he walked away. Where are you going with this, Hannah?"

"All I'm saying is he must feel something for you— something strong enough to make him fight for *you* instead of just replacing you. Let's face it, he's rich, easy on the eyes and from what you've said, a god in bed. He wouldn't have any trouble finding other women to warm his sheets. But he wants you. If you still love him, why not fight for him?"

"Maybe he just hates to be dumped instead of being the one doing the dumping."

"Maybe. And maybe he can't stand the thought of letting you go."

"But he's engaged to *her* and that's not going to change."

"He's not married yet. And that article you showed me said he's known her for years. *Years.* Did you believe him when he said he hadn't slept with her?"

Had she? Yes. She'd seen the truth in his eyes. "Yes."

"It's not as if he hasn't had the opportunity to make it legal before now. Seems like he's not all that eager to spend time with her—in bed or out—if you know what I mean."

Megan gnawed her lip and considered her cousin's theory. It made sense. Sort of. "I hear what you're saying, but…"

"Let me put it another way—and good grief, I can't believe I'm actually arguing for the bastard—you've lost him already. What more do you have to lose by fighting just a teensy bit harder?"

"My baby. Another piece of my heart."

"And how will *not* fighting for him change that?"

A sinking sensation settled over her. "Good point. I hate it when you're right."

"All you need to do is make him realize all the things you can give him that Mademoiselle Prissy Pants Debussey cannot."

The spark of hope—along with a heavy dose of competitive spirit—caught and blazed to life inside Megan. Tapping a finger to her lip, she paced the break room.

Why not try to win him back? But she'd have to be

careful, because the higher the jump, the harder the fall. And the more she allowed herself to believe this crazy scheme had a chance of working, the more it would hurt if she failed.

"I'm going to need a foolproof plan."

Megan shoved a spoonful of Ben & Jerry's Clusterfluff ice cream into her mouth and stepped back to contemplate the three columns of sticky notes she'd attached to her refrigerator door.

A visual map of her strategy always helped her clarify her thoughts, and while she'd only used this method of attack on her competitors before, it couldn't hurt to try it in her bid to win Xavier.

She rolled a sweet caramel cluster around in her mouth and debated plan A. The vertical row of pink squares was by far her first choice, the plan that would make everything right in her world and restore her previous fairy-tale romance state.

On the first square she'd written, "Get Xavier to choose me."

The black scrawl on the second patch said, "Convince him to ditch his fiancée by enlightening him to their differences and C's deficiencies."

The third, "Show X we are perfect outside of bed as well as in and that I am truly an asset, his other half."

Next, "Facilitate introductions to powerful connections."

And last, "Anticipate and provide any nonsexual needs."

She took another spoonful, this time savoring the rich peanut butter and fluffy marshmallow swirls on her tongue. "The question is, how?"

What could she do that she wasn't doing already? She stabbed the spoon into the pint and set aside her comfort food, then pulled the marker from behind her ear and picked up the pink pad. Pen poised, she stared at the sheet. But her mind went as blank as the page on the implementation. She'd have to come back to that one.

"Moving right along," she muttered as she dropped the pen and pink pad, retrieved her ice cream and focused on the blue row that stretched five sticky notes long. Plan B. An option she'd rather avoid because it was risky. Scary. It made her vulnerable and therefore opened her to more pain. Even her writing was more rigid on this collection of squares, her tension over this particular course revealed by thicker lines as if she'd pressed the Sharpie a bit too hard on the paper.

"X believes our relationship is *only* about sex. Prove him wrong by:

"Giving him only sex.

"Withhold all intellectual nonsexual communication.

"No cuddling, breakfasts in bed or other tender couple activities that he apparently takes for granted.

"No spontaneous touching or hand-holding."

The last one would be tough since she loved sharing all those things with him. But if it was the only way to win the war...

Agitation built in her stomach. She gobbled a double shovel of ice cream to soothe it before moving on to the yellow row. Plan C was the worst-case scenario and the shortest column—only one forlorn square inscribed with a shaky hand.

"Raise baby alone."

Plan C was worse than being disqualified from a show. Heartbreaking. Humiliating. A waste of so much potential.

A knock on the front door followed by the sound of it opening pierced her concentration. Only Hannah or Xavier would let themselves in without waiting for her to answer.

"Megan!"

Xavier.

His voice acted like a starting gun to her heart rate, accelerating it wildly. She couldn't let him come back here and see this blueprint. She dumped the ice cream and pen on the table and sprinted for the den, then skidded to a halt on the hardwood floor at the sight of him. Her already racing heart hammered faster.

"What are you doing here?"

His eyes narrowed. "Is something wrong?"

"Not at all. Why?"

"You are breathless and…" He tilted his head assessingly. "You look guilty." He moved forward.

She gulped but held her ground, blocking the path to the kitchen. He stopped so close she could smell his cologne and feel the heat radiating off his body. Warmth rushed her face. "Guilty? Of what? It's almost ten o'clock. What could I be doing this late at night?"

A wicked glint—a sexual spark—entered his eyes, making her blood thicken with desire, then his gaze locked on her mouth and her lungs stalled. Would he kiss her? Could she—*should she*—resist? He lifted a hand. His thumb skimmed the corner of her mouth, stirring up all kinds of hormonal trouble—the kind that could make her resolutions bite the dust.

"Guilty of satisfying your sweet tooth." He licked his finger and smiled, and her heart swooped like a barn swallow diving for dinner. "Peanut butter ice cream?"

"Yeah, so?"

"Do you have lessons to teach this weekend?"

She blinked at the abrupt change of subject. "Lessons? No. Most of my students are visiting a small local show. I was going to go with them."

"Good." He turned on his heel and grasped the doorknob.

"Why?"

"I'll see you tomorrow, *mon amante*. Sleep well."

"But why—?"

The door clicked behind him. Frustrated by his non-answer, she debated going after him but decided to let him go. The last thing she needed was to spend time with him before she'd finished working out her strategy. Especially now when he'd aroused her without even trying.

"That was weird," she muttered to herself, then locked the door and returned to the kitchen. She had a lot of fine-tuning to do before she saw him again. But first she needed a cold shower.

Xavier could not afford to have a bastard child. Doing so would undermine the honor he had worked so hard to restore to the Alexandre name. He had lived with the whispers, the furtive glances, the pointing fingers. Even though times had changed and single parenthood was more accepted, he would not risk his child suffering that fate.

He walked the short distance from his temporary home to the stables while debating his options. As Megan had pointed out, Haithcock Farm was not up to his standards, but, surprisingly, now that the repairs had been completed, the house and the furniture included in the lease were comfortable.

The small property would not require the extensive staff his larger estate required—a bonus since he had neither the time nor interest in conducting numerous interviews for what would be a short stay. The four-man crew he had hired would suffice.

But what made the property the most attractive was its proximity to Megan. However, the tall pines bordering the rolling green pastures were so thick that he could not see Sutherland Farm even though it was but a short jog away.

To see Megan, he had to get into his car instead of simply being able to look out his study window as he did at home.

That brought his thoughts back to the woman at the center of his current problem. Megan. She was proving her stubbornness each day. But his new stable manager had called to say Megan had come for an unannounced visit this morning. Xavier considered that progress. Her presence would save him a trip to Sutherland Farm later.

Providing for Megan's child financially and walking away as she had asked would be merely covering the issue with sand and hoping a strong wind would not reveal it at a later date. Even if he raised the child with Cecille, he could not risk Megan changing her mind years from now and trying to reclaim their child the way his mother had done. His mother had shown up when Xavier was twelve declaring she'd made a mistake and wanted to be a mother to her only son.

Ten years too late. And of course, she had not experienced this motherly urge until her lover had dumped her for a younger woman and Xavier's father had turned the company's finances around. His father had wanted to allow her back into their lives, but Xavier had convinced him that she had abandoned them once and would likely do so again. His father had not been happy, but he had sent his ex-wife away.

Xavier had just one choice. Legitimizing his child by whatever means necessary was the only way to avoid scandal and keep Megan from returning. He must find a way to persuade her to relinquish her claim.

But what would it take? Everyone had a price. What was Megan's? In the past, he had offered her jewelry and even a horse that had caught her eye, but she had declined each gift. The only items she had accepted were of no consequence—clothing required for the high-society events she attended with him and furnishings for the cottage she shared with him.

He sifted through memories of past conversations for clues and realized the majority of their discussions had centered on horses—his, hers, the competition's. Incendiary sex did not require words and much of their shared time had been spent preparing for, engaging in or recovering from the activity.

He knew very little of her childhood except that she had lost her family when she was thirteen. Their home had been sold and she had been forced to reside with her uncle who had made her unwelcome. She had shared little else.

He scanned the Bermuda pastures that had somehow survived years of neglect and then focused on the cedar and stone house. Perhaps a home of her own would tempt her.

He spotted Megan by the riding ring and his pulse quickened with the desire for her that time and distance had not quenched. He did not understand her hold on him. But it would pass. It must.

He barely spared a glance at the young man riding Apollo. Timothy had talent, but alas could not compete at Megan's level. Instead Xavier focused on the mother of his child. How could he have missed the significance of the new—and very alluring—fullness of Megan's breasts, the slight swelling of her belly, the radiance of her skin?

Pregnancy agreed with her. And he could not remember ever having thought that about any woman before.

Convincing Megan to return to France with him was no longer an option. As she had said, flagrantly parading his pregnant mistress in front of his fiancée would only create more controversy. Megan's abrupt departure from the show circuit had already been noted. She was ranked high enough to catch the gossips' curiosity by vanishing.

He would have to remain in the States until he could convince her to relinquish his heir.

A slight breeze teased the hair flowing down Megan's back like a midnight waterfall. Previously she had worn it loose only during and after sex when the tangled strands caressed her shoulders or draped his pillowcase. She usually preferred it "out of the way," she claimed.

He knew her well enough to know the copper highlights streaking the dark locks resulted from sun exposure rather than a skilled hairdresser. Megan was one of the few women he had encountered who did not rely on the cosmetic industry for her beauty. Her lack of artifice had been part of her appeal.

"*Bonjour, chérie.* What brings you to my stables this morning?"

"Good morning." Her smile, as always, lightened his mood. "I came to help Tim with Apollo."

Her blue sleeveless top intensified the hue of her eyes, and her fuller breasts strained the fabric, providing a glimpse of her plain cotton bra between the gaping button plackets. The combination made it difficult for Xavier to remember his agenda.

Get her back in his bed and then he would have the next six months to convince her to grant him full custody. He doubted it would take that long once he pointed out the advantages of relinquishing the baby.

"Timothy does not have your gift with horses."

"It's not a gift. It's experience. All he needs is saddle time."

"I disagree. Watching you ride is like listening to a fine orchestra. You are in tune with your mounts, finessing each nuance of movement." She was the same with him, never missing an opportunity to magnify his response with a subtle squeeze, a different angle, a touch.

He blamed the sweat beading his skin on the unrelenting sun beating down. And knew he lied.

For a moment, her gaze held his with the same tenderness she used to show before the article had surfaced. Then she bit her lip and returned her attention to the ring. It was not until she looked away that he realized he'd missed her adoration. Her love. How had he not recognized the feelings written so clearly on her face?

Because you did not want to.

Her hand trembled slightly as she tucked a glossy lock behind her ear. "Tim's one of Sutherland Farm's best amateurs. If you want a better rider you'll have to hire a professional, but our pro riders are contracted to their maximum number of clients. You could always transfer your horses to another stable or take them home."

He ignored her not-so-subtle invitation to leave the country. "*Non.* You are here."

He caught a slight hitch in her breath. "I'd like to help Tim with your horses. I know those animals as well as I know my own. I can help you maintain their value by coaching him. You might even get a few ribbons before the show season ends."

Having her here would definitely work to his advantage. "You are welcome at my home anytime, Megan. May I?"

He didn't wait for permission before placing his hand across her lower abdomen. She startled and would have moved away had he not anchored her by hooking his other arm around her waist.

"What are you doing?"

The breathless quality of her voice resembled the way she cried out his name when he feasted on her. Heat and pressure built within him like steam in a still.

Mon dieu. Would this hunger for her never abate? He ached to slide his hand into her pants and stroke the warm curve of her belly, to delve into the soft curls and slick folds below. His mouth watered for a taste of her.

As if reading his thoughts she shifted uneasily. Had he not been intimately acquainted with her body, he would not have noticed the extra firmness beneath her navel.

He corralled his salacious thoughts. "Like any good *papa,* I wish to be a part of your pregnancy and to see your body bloom with my child."

"*Our* child. What about Parfums Alexandre? Who's going to run your company while you're away?"

"I will contact the appropriate people to arrange a satellite office in the house." He caressed the denim covering their *bébé.* "Move in with me, Megan, and let us share this miraculous occasion."

She gasped and for a brief moment he saw temptation in her eyes. She twisted out of reach, but the flush on her cheeks and the quickened pulse fluttering in her neck revealed she was as affected as he by the contact.

"I'd like for you to be a part of my pregnancy. But I won't move in with you."

"Why do you deny us both the wealth of pleasure we could find in each other's arms? I miss the satin of your skin next to mine, *mon amante,* and the hot, sweet embrace of your body."

Her lips parted and her eyes turned slumberous and he thought he had her, but then she shook her head and hugged her middle. "I need to get used to living without you."

Living without him. The words punctured his skin like a dull hypodermic needle. But she was right. The day would come when they must part. But that was months away.

"I am going to contact the owners about purchasing Haithcock Farm."

Her eyes narrowed. "Why would you do that? You have a perfectly fine estate in France."

And after the wedding he would have two estates. "The property will be my gift to you once you have signed custody of the child over to me. You will have a home base near your cousin."

Hurt flickered across her face. "What good is a home without a family to share it? How many times and how many ways do I have to say I'm not giving up my baby? You can't bribe me into changing my mind with a piece of land or a pot of money."

"It is more than land. I am offering you security and the opportunity to return to the competition you love without the hindrance of a child."

"Competition isn't the most important thing in my life anymore. My baby is. If you insist, you can visit him or her."

She proved more *obstinée* than he had expected. "My heir must be taught the Alexandre business from the soonest moment he can comprehend his heritage."

"Be indoctrinated in duty and honor, you mean? Look how well that's working for you. You're going to marry someone you claim you care nothing about for the sake of Parfums Alexandre."

"The marriage is not about money. The money is irrelevant."

"Spoken like someone who's never had to worry about whether or not he can pay the rent or put food on the table. Tell me something, Xavier. How much do you know about your bride-to-be other than the fact that her father is pushing her into an arranged marriage and she's meek enough to agree?"

The attack surprised him. "It is not like you to be catty, Megan."

"No. But it *is* like me to study my competition and assess their strengths and weaknesses, and nothing I've learned about Cecille indicates she'll be a good wife to you or, heaven forbid, a decent stepmother to my child.

"She's a party girl. Did you know that? Late nights overindulging in booze have never been your thing. You're a man who treats a cocktail party like a military campaign. You connect with the people you've predetermined to be important. Once that's done, you leave. You never linger and you're never the last to leave. You certainly never drink enough to lose your wits.

"And Cecille must love getting her picture in the tabloids because I found hundreds of images of her when I did an internet search on her name. You like your privacy, and you hate being written about in the tabloids."

"Cecille will conduct herself appropriately after the marriage—as I will."

"Are you sure? Did you know she's an avid tennis fan and religiously attends Grand Slam matches worldwide? You hate tennis, and from what I read, she's not fond of horses. What will you have in common?"

"Those are minor details which we will work out."

"She's twenty-five and she's never had a job."

"My wife need not work."

"No, but she needs to be interested in more than just fashion and tennis to hold your attention."

"Are you quite finished with your assassination of her character?"

"I'm sorry. I'm not trying to be argumentative or insult someone I've never met, but I don't think you're looking at the big picture. Other than both of your fathers starting perfume manufacturing companies and French citizenship you have little in common."

Her arguments were beginning to irritate him— primarily because they pinpointed every negative aspect of the marriage arrangement. But he had no alternative.

He'd sworn on his father's grave that he would right all the wrongs his father had committed—the most important being the loss of the Alexandre estate. The only way to regain the property was to marry Cecille. Her father had turned down every purchase offer Xavier had made.

But now that Megan had planted the seed of doubt, Xavier had to wonder why Monsieur Debussey had insisted on marriage. And why Cecille had agreed.

"I assure you, I am cognizant of the situation. But that is months away. What is important immediately is that I have registered the horses in the show in Lexington this weekend."

"That's why you asked if I had students?"

"Oui."

"Couldn't we start with the smaller local show? Tim isn't ready for that level of competition."

"But the horses are and Tim must learn."

"You must've pulled some strings to make that happen on short notice."

"Providing sponsorship and prize money can be very persuasive. You will attend with me."

She hesitated. "I don't think it's a good idea for you to be seen with me when you just announced your engagement. There will be photographers swarming at a show of that size."

"Paparazzo? I think not."

"Equestrian magazine people. A show of this size always has a good write-up in the important publications."

"No one in the States cares about my personal affairs."

"Are you kidding me? When the CEO of one of the world's top perfumeries becomes engaged to the daughter of his strongest rival, it's news."

"If you will not attend the show for me, then do so for Timothy. He will need your guidance."

"You've asked him about this?"

He dipped his head. "He is eager to test his skills against a more competitive field."

She grimaced, glanced at horse and rider, tapped her toe, then sighed and he knew he had her. "I want my own hotel room."

"Do you not remember our nights—"

"I remember. But I still want my own room."

"As you wish." He bowed slightly.

He would acquiesce this time. But that did not mean he would not try to change her mind. He wanted Megan back in his bed. But more than that, he was counting on her stint in the stands at the show making her yearn to return to the competition she loved. Then she would see that there was no room in her life for a child.

Five

Megan followed the bellhop into the luxurious hotel room. Xavier shadowing her steps was her first inkling that all was not as she'd requested.

She stopped and scanned the space. One elegant sitting room. Two bedrooms—one on either side—both with king-size beds visible through the open doors. Nothing subtle about that.

"This is a suite. I asked for my own room."

"That will be all." Xavier tipped the hotel employee and sent him on his way, then indicated the open door to the left. "You have your own room."

"That's not what I meant and you know it. You should have put me in the same hotel as Tim."

"Tim is staying with the rest of the equestrian team in a hotel closer to the show grounds. Megan, rest assured, I will not force my attentions on you."

He'd never had to force her into anything. That was part of the problem. Around him, her strong will vanished.

He checked his watch. "We have limited time before our first engagement of the evening. Since you left your evening wear in Grasse, I have arranged appropriate cocktail attire for you. It should be in your room. We will leave in thirty minutes."

He strode into the room on the right and, without closing the door behind him, removed his coat and tie, tossing them on the bed. Megan turned away from the sight of him disrobing and debated insisting on a different room, but she had an agenda for the weekend. Creating friction now wouldn't help her cause.

A moment later, she heard his shower turn on. Desire instantly percolated inside her. Memories of hot shared showers pushed themselves forward.

But that was plan B. First she had to give plan A a chance to work.

She deliberately marched into her room. After closing and locking her door she headed for the closet and discovered a garment bag emblazoned with a very familiar logo—that of her favorite Parisian designer. Xavier had always claimed this particular designer fashioned clothing as if she had intimate knowledge of Megan's body. A smaller bag sat on the shelf above and a shoe box rested on the floor below.

Eagerness Megan had no business feeling fizzed through her. Xavier hadn't told her anything except they'd be attending two cocktail parties on the show grounds.

She felt a twinge of reservation about accepting more expensive gifts from him, but she hadn't brought anything suitable with her from France, and the dress she'd borrowed from Hannah wouldn't be the haute couture expected at the kind of gatherings Xavier usually frequented.

Xavier seemed to take pleasure in dressing Megan for the occasion, and when she was with him she fit into any celebrity, designer-draped crowd. It looked as though tonight would follow the same pattern, and if she wanted to prove she was perfect for him, then she needed to dress the part.

She opened the smallest bag first and discovered a decadently fragile bra and panty set in rich purple. Next she unzipped the garment bag and her breath caught. The midnight-blue cocktail dress had an almost iridescent sheen. She stroked the soft, glimmering material then laid the dress on the bed and went back to the closet for the shoes. She fell in love the moment she opened the box and saw the nude color crisscross leather sandals with mountain-high heels. *Très* sexy.

She quickly touched up her makeup then stripped off her clothes and donned the lingerie. Sheer lace provided glimpses of her aureoles and the curls between her legs. Her heart pumped harder. She looked good in these. So good she wished Xavier could see her.

Uh-uh. Plan B again.

Pushing that thought aside, she slipped the silky jersey knit over her head and added the shoes. She stepped in front of the mirror and twisted left then right. Wow. The fabric shimmered from navy to almost purple in the changing light. It deepened the color of her eyes and made her skin look luminous.

The wrapped bodice dipped low, revealing more cleavage than she was accustomed to, but then she had more cleavage to reveal than she used to because her pregnancy had made her breasts a full cup size larger. And somehow Xavier had known that. The bra and dress fit perfectly.

The short, ruched, tulip-hemmed skirt fell just shy of midthigh, making the most of her figure and showcasing her legs while concealing her budding belly. No one would suspect her secret in this miracle of a dress.

Oh, Xavier, you do know how to dress your women.

She smiled. Little did he know he'd inadvertently given Plan A a huge boost. Plan B, too. This dress provided powerful ammunition for either strategy. And when she looked this good, plan C—raising her child alone—would never come into play.

This horse show weekend was her time to shine, her opportunity to prove to Xavier that they were an unbeatable pair, that having her by his side made his life better and easier.

As soon as he'd told her they were attending the show, she'd employed her talent for remembering minutiae and gone online to study the major players—the sponsors, owners, exhibitors and horses.

If things went according to her playbook, before they returned home Sunday night, Xavier would no longer be able to deny that she was an asset he couldn't afford to lose.

Money, Megan decided, smelled the same on every continent, and she was surrounded by it.

Adrenaline pumped through her veins as she carefully made her way in her new heels through the show grounds beside Xavier. Heads turned as they passed. Xavier's tall, athletic grace and good looks always drew attention, but put him in a custom-made dinner jacket and lascivious looks from the women and a few of the men never failed to follow.

She couldn't help but be proud to be seen with a man who could have any woman he wanted. And knowing she looked damned good, too, didn't hurt her confidence or her plan any.

But truth be told, even though she'd been raised on the

Grand Prix circuit and her father had been a high-ranked rider, she was more comfortable consorting with the carrot man, the freelance braiders or any of the other peddlers pushing their horse- and dog-related wares.

"You are very quiet this evening," Xavier said, interrupting her thoughts.

"I'm just remembering the days when my brother and I spent most of our time with the vendors. Since the same group often frequents the same shows and my mom made friends with most of them, the vendors were like extended family. Did I ever tell you my first job was braiding manes and tails?"

"*Non.* You have said little about your family."

"Dad was the equestrian. Mom packed us up and we followed him to every show. We weren't vagabonds at all. We were a family. A tight unit."

"Your father could not have been the one to teach you how to interact with sponsors if he died when you were a teen."

"And you can bet my uncle didn't. I picked that up on my own. Competing is expensive business, and I've never been independently wealthy. I learned to mingle at the cocktail parties and the fancy chef-prepared buffets to pick up sponsors. It took a while but eventually I mastered the art of not getting star-struck and stammering around the rich and famous."

"I have never seen you less than poised."

She'd have to be *more* than poised tonight if she wanted to prove she was perfect for him.

Golf carts, some privately owned, some rented from the onsite vendor, zipped past, making their way toward the tent kingdom ahead, which housed owners, exhibitors, dignitaries and upscale vendors selling everything from jewelry to tack to gourmet dog biscuits.

"When I was a child I believed the show grounds resembled something from the Arabian Nights, with each stable having its own brightly colored drapes and awnings. But that's where the fairy tale stopped. I never dreamed of a prince. I always dreamed of the perfect horse."

Xavier's hand enclosed hers and he gave her an indulgent smile. Megan's pulse skipped. She rested her cheek against his shoulder as she'd done a thousand times before, then she remembered they weren't on hand-holding terms anymore. Not yet anyway. She straightened and tried to pull free, but he held fast, tugging her against his lean, hard body as a cart passed too close.

"Careful, *chérie*."

Falling back into their old relationship, into his arms and his bed would be so easy. But that was plan B. "I should probably swing by the exhibitor tent to check on Tim. This is his first big show. He's probably a nervous wreck."

"Tim is in the capable hands of the stable's equestrian team. He is fine. You are here as an owner this time, Megan, not an exhibitor. You will stay with me."

"I'm here as an owner only because you paid the exorbitant entry fees for my horses."

"As you have said, you cannot devalue the animals by removing them from competition."

"But three thousand per horse—"

"It is done. We have reached our first event of the evening." He stopped in front of a massive white-and-cobalt tent. The entrance was an intricately designed flower garden complete with a gurgling water fountain, twinkling lights and a violinist to welcome the new arrivals. "Smile, *mon amante*. No woman here can possibly be as beautiful as you tonight."

When he looked at her like he wanted her—*only* her—

she melted a little and her carefully constructed strategies blurred. "Thank you."

He withdrew an embossed ivory invitation from his pocket and handed it to the tuxedoed guard. The man checked his list then waved them through. Megan scanned the crowd, spotting at least four movie stars, a presidential candidate and the TV chef she'd been watching late at night when she couldn't sleep.

Their hostess, a blonde beauty who'd recently inherited a world-renowned jewelry company, left a fashion icon behind to greet them.

"Xavier, darling, it's good to see you stateside again. I'm so glad you could come to my little soiree," she said before kissing him full on the mouth. When she withdrew she lingered over wiping her lipstick from his lips until Xavier adroitly maneuvered out of reach by pulling Megan forward.

The woman's gaze chilled substantially when she focused on Megan. "I hear congratulations are in order. Is this your fiancée?"

An icy splash of humiliation washed over Megan.

Xavier stiffened almost imperceptibly. If his arm hadn't been pressed against her she wouldn't have noticed. "*Non*. Renee, may I present Megan Sutherland? She has been riding my horses and her own on the European Circuit. Quite successfully."

The woman's exquisitely made-up eyes reassessed Megan and dismissed her as if a lowly equestrian were beneath her notice. "Are you riding tomorrow?"

"No. I'm taking the rest of the season off to help my cousin plan her wedding. One of our up-and-coming riders will be competing on the horses."

Xavier's palm branded on Megan's spine. "Megan has generously agreed to act as trainer and assist him."

"How kind of you," Renee said in a saccharine tone that implied she couldn't care less. "Where is your bride-to-be, darling? I so want to meet the woman who has brought Xavier Alexandre to heel."

The hostess's bitterness made Megan wonder if she and Xavier had a history, but it was the underlying message in the not-so-subtle dig that reminded Megan how small the global equestrian community could be. No matter which continent she competed on, it would be impossible to avoid news of Xavier, his wife and any children they might have. That meant her plan had to work. Preferably plan A, because plan B was dicey.

Grateful for the research she'd done on her competition, she forced a big smile for her hostess. "The French Open is this weekend, and Cecille is a devoted tennis fan. I would wager my best horse that she has center court seats."

The quick flash of surprise and approval in Xavier's eyes rewarded her. "That is correct."

Megan had ridden sick and she'd ridden hurt. Pasting a plastic smile on her face and faking for the judges was nothing new. Contending for the man she loved at a cocktail party shouldn't be all that different. There was no doubt in her mind that this was a jump-off between her and Cecille, even though the other woman wasn't on American soil. And the clock was ticking. Megan had to give a faultless performance.

But she always rode to win, and there was no better way to prove to Xavier that she was the woman he needed than by playing up their mutual love of horses and the fact that she was by his side while his fiancée was not.

Funny how dread and anticipation shared similar indicators: rapid pulse, quickened breaths, moistened palms.

Megan lagged a half pace behind Xavier as he strolled

down the carpeted hotel corridor with his I-own-the-world swagger. She had been dreading this part of the evening—the same part she'd once anticipated the most.

Would Xavier try to kiss her? Invite her into his room? And if he did, would she stick with plan A, the safest strategy, and keep trying to show him how much they had going for them besides sex?

Or would she step up her game and go to the much riskier and more complicated plan B?

On one hand, he'd had her hyperactive hormones simmering all night. Each glance had stolen her breath and each touch had been like a tiny electrical shock. And he never *just* touched. He made contact, then skimmed his fingertips an inch or two across her skin—far enough to give her goose bumps. Spending the rest of the night in his arms would be extremely satisfying. Physically.

But plan B—showing him that they had so much more going for them by giving him sex and only sex then walking away—demanded more control than she'd ever displayed in her life. It would require her to keep her heart out of their lovemaking and focus solely on the physical aspects.

Using the passion between them to sway him was a strategy as old as time, but his rejection after they'd made love in her cottage had left her reeling, hurt and empty. She wasn't sure she wanted to go there again—even if it might be the most effective line of attack.

She followed Xavier into the suite, then shifted uneasily on her feet at the threshold of her room. She waited for his next move, but he made no attempt to talk his way into her bed. Just as well. She wasn't convinced plan B would work, and it would leave devastation in its wake if it failed.

"Well…good night, then. I guess I should get some sleep. Big day tomorrow."

"Tim's first event is not until eleven. You and I shall share breakfast before making our way to the grounds."

In the past they'd awoken together, showered together and sometimes made love before she raced to the show grounds, her muscles all loose and warm, her skin still tingling from his caresses. The memories sent a rush of heat through her. "I was hoping to meet with Tim and go over his game plan one more time."

"Megan, *ma petit concourante,* you have prepared him as best you can. Give him time to digest your advice and plot his own course."

"But—"

"Breakfast will be delivered at eight." He strode into his room as if assured of her acceptance.

Megan walked into her room and shut the door. The second the latch caught, she sagged against the panel. Was she actually disappointed Xavier hadn't made a move on her? Yes. She wanted to make love with him, wanted to hold him and be held by him. Wanted *him,* damn it. But she wanted it the way it used to be. Correction, the way she had believed it to be when she'd been oblivious to his long-range plans. She wanted her fairy-tale romance back.

Why was he making this a contest between her and Cecille?

She forced her feet into motion, moving by rote through her usual routine of undressing, showering and putting on her camisole and tap pants—lacy French remnants from her days with Xavier—not that he'd ever let her sleep in the garments. But having him remove them was half the fun.

Too keyed up to sleep, too aware of the man on the other side of the locked door and totally disappointed by her indecisiveness, she perched on the edge of her bed, picked

up the TV remote and clicked through the channels just
to fill the silence.

Her stomach growled. Despite the sumptuous buffets
they'd attended, working the parties wasn't conducive to
eating. She rarely did more than nibble a few bites. She'd
have to call room service. She reached for the phone and
spotted the clock. After midnight. Would the kitchens be
open? The luxury hotels Xavier preferred tended to be a
little more accommodating for their high-paying customers.
She might be in luck.

A knock made her jump. Had that come from the hall
door or the adjoining room? She turned off the television.
A second knock spurred her pulse into a stampede. Xavier
was calling.

Finding the right balance between making him want
more without giving too much of herself wasn't going to
be easy. She detoured by the bathroom, pulled on the thick
hotel robe and tied it tightly around her middle.

She inhaled a game-on breath and opened the door.
Xavier's still-damp hair told her he'd also showered, but
he wore jeans and V-neck shirt instead of the silk pajama
bottoms he usually donned at this time of night. His attire
threw her. If he'd shown up looking like a walking sex
machine she'd have had an inkling what he wanted.

His green eyes raked over her, the pupils expanding
as if he could see the delicate lingerie beneath the heavy
white terry cloth. A reciprocal hunger echoed deep inside
her. How many post-party nights had they made love until
exhaustion claimed them? She missed sleeping in his arms
and hearing the slow and steady thump of his heart beneath
her ear—a lover's lullaby.

"Did you need something, Xavier?"

"Dinner waits." He swept an arm to indicate the silver
dome-laden table by the window of the sitting room.

"Dinner?" Her mouth dried.

"I am sure you are as ravenous as always after the preshow events."

He had her there. And if she spent time with him she might be able to figure out this unfamiliar move of his. "I could eat."

He crossed the room and lifted the first shiny dome. Tacos? She blinked and a laugh bubbled out. She'd expected champagne and seduction. "Not your usual gourmet fare."

A smile teased his lips. "It always amused me that you could sit in a five-star restaurant and reminisce of American junk food." He removed the remaining lids and set them aside, melting her heart like mozzarella in a pizza oven as he uncovered each dish.

"I have ordered corn dogs, barbecue, fried onion rings, New York cheesecake with fresh berries and of course, lemonade. Have I covered all of your food fantasies, *mon amante?*"

She fell a little deeper in love with him in that moment. She looked from the smorgasbord of her all-time favorites to the man she craved more than any of them. Hope sparked in her chest.

"Yes." The single word was all she could choke out.

Xavier never let a detail slip when something mattered to him and whether he realized it or not, he'd just proven he cared about her by including all the foods she'd yammered about during their very first date when she'd been so nervous around the sexy, suave Frenchman that she couldn't stop talking.

She wasn't giving him up without a fight.

Even if it meant fighting dirty—something she never, *ever* did.

* * *

Something had changed during the course of the meal. Xavier was not sure what exactly. But he liked it.

Megan's lips had relaxed from their previously tight line, and when their gazes met, hers lingered instead of bouncing away as it had since he had tracked her to the States.

Her relaxed state could not be attributed to wine since in deference to her pregnancy he had abstained from contacting the sommelier to ask what to serve with the State Fair meal they had consumed. Probably moonshine—the potent beverage Xavier had sampled compliments of an acquaintance who had settled in rural Georgia to establish a winery.

That same *confrère* had introduced Xavier to Renee nine years ago. Xavier could not regret his subsequent affair with the jewelry heiress since it had exposed him to horses and Grand Prix competition that he now enjoyed. And his interest in horses had led him to Megan. But Renee's bitchiness tonight had reminded him why he had ended their relationship after only a few months.

"Mmm. Mmm. Mmm." Megan patted her stomach, leaned back in her seat and smiled like a satisfied woman. Her actions pulled his thoughts away from the old flame he had no intention of rekindling despite the hotel key card and note Renee had slipped into his pocket earlier.

"Thank you, Xavier. That was stupendously good."

For him, as well. Watching Megan eat had been a purely sensual experience—like exquisitely drawn-out foreplay. "I am happy the meal pleased you."

"I probably shouldn't have eaten so much, but my appetite has been almost insatiable lately. I had to try everything."

The words *insatiable* and *appetite* falling from her lips

made his heart pound. Oh, yes, his Megan did have a very healthy sexual appetite.

He pushed his barely touched plate aside. He had consumed enough of the food to satisfy one hunger. Now he would slake the other. "I have missed these quiet moments with you."

A combination of wariness and need filled her eyes. "Me, too. And the idea of not having any more of these nights…"

She dipped her head and her hair cascaded forward to hide her expression. Regret twisted inside him. He hated that she would be hurt. But what choice did he have?

He rose, walked behind her chair and gently brushed her hair over one shoulder. The dark strands slid through his fingers like cool, heavy satin. He moved the collar of her robe out of the way and lightly grazed his nails over her nape the way he knew she liked. She shivered as expected and goose bumps lifted her smooth, ivory flesh.

"I want you, *mon amante*. I want to sleep with you in my arms, with the taste of you on my lips and the scent of you clinging to my skin."

Her dense lashes descended and after a moment her head tilted in invitation. He bent and inhaled, drawing the essence of her into his lungs and imbedding it into his memory. He dusted a necklace of featherlight kisses across her shoulders and nape.

Her breath shuddered in then out again. "Why me?"

She had asked him the same question the first time he had invited her to dinner. "Because we share a passion that cannot be denied."

He had recognized the force of it from the moment their eyes had met at a pre-event sponsor party—just as he'd known she would be his as soon as he had discovered she was as career-focused as he. But he had not expected his thirst for her to be unquenchable. At some point, he would get his fill. He must. But not yet.

He pulled her chair away from the table. She hesitated a moment then rose and turned. He untied the knot at her waist and pushed her robe from her shoulders. She shrugged, letting it fall to the floor. Her nipples tented the lacy lavender camisole and desire pulsed in his groin. He circled one bead with his fingertip, making it tighten and rise even more.

Passion filled her face with dusky color. Her back bowed, encouraging and inviting him. His second hand joined the first, brushing, plucking, rolling until the silk between his flesh and hers warmed. He palmed the weight of her breasts through the fabric, but the obstructed contact was insufficient. He needed to touch her skin, to taste her.

He whisked her top over her head. Her increased size enraptured him. "Your dress tonight—" Desire thickened his throat. "You looked *incroyable.* No man could keep his eyes off you."

He'd been jealous. Territorial. And ravenous for her. He had barely paid attention to the potentially influential connections he had made. His mind had been focused on her dress—and how to remove it.

He adored everything about a woman's shape, but usually legs—Megan's were exceptional—caught his attention. But tonight the soft, pale globes had transfixed him from the moment she had opened her bedroom door. How had he never noticed the slight blue veining beneath her translucent skin? He traced each line, first with a fingertip and then, because he could not resist, with his tongue, making her gasp and squirm.

He buried his face in the ivory valley and inhaled the heady scent unique to Megan. His perfumer instincts yearned for the skill to bottle her *arôme magnifique.* If he could sell the effect she had on him, he would be rich beyond even his father's wildest dreams. Richer than he would be once he merged with Parfums Debussey.

Her fingers threaded through his hair, holding him close and guiding him toward a sensitive peak. He sucked her deep into his mouth, savoring her flavor and her quiet whimpers of approval. He feasted on her breasts, then her soft lips and slick tongue. When his hunger rose too swiftly, he retreated, gasping for air, to the cords of her neck. But the repast was not enough.

He needed to taste the dew of her desire, feel the intimate embrace of her body. He swept her into his arms and carried her to his bedroom. The maid had already turned back the covers of the king-size bed. He lowered Megan onto the sheets. Part of him expected her to object. After all, she had been denying him since that explosive welcome in her cottage. But no protests came. He was beyond caring why she had changed her mind.

Instead she rolled to her side, stroked the sheets and watched him, waiting for him with her damp lips parted and her magnificent breasts rising and falling with quickened breaths. He ripped off his clothing, then lowered her silk bottoms down her legs. For a moment he could only stare at her, drinking in the beauty of her womanly shape lying in his bed.

Then his overpowering need took precedence. He stretched out on the cool sheets beside her, pulling her hot body flush against his. The contact smote him with a flash fire of urgency.

He had once taken such a simple embrace for granted, but never again. He paused to savor having her as close as they could be without their bodies being intimately joined. The wild rhythm of her heart hastened his own. The slow glide of her palm over his biceps and her calf sliding up the outside of his leg stretched his restraint to near breaking point.

She outlined his ear with a delicate fingertip, traced his bottom lip with her tongue and pressed her breasts to his chest. Megan had never been shy in bed, but tonight she seemed more audacious as she alternately massaged his shoulders, back and buttocks with firm hands, then dusted her fingers over his skin. The contrast of hard and soft propelled him far too quickly toward the edge of reason and self-control.

He reminded himself that she carried his child. He must rein in the feral response lest he hurt her and *le bébé*.

He caught her hands and lifted them to the pillow above her head, then straddled her hips. Holding her captive, he bent and kissed her temple, her nose, her mouth. Her lips parted offering him more, but he diverted to her jaw, her ear, her neck and finally her resplendent breasts. She twisted beneath him, tormenting him with each flexing, writhing muscle. But he would not be rushed. Not when the hourglass counted down the number of nights he had left with her. He would make this one last.

Keeping her hands locked in his, he knelt between her legs, opening her, exposing her, then he sipped his way down her torso and anchored her wrists by her hips. He tongued her navel, nuzzled the triangle of dark curls and found the nectar he sought. She cried out. Her hips arched in invitation. He teased her everywhere but where he knew she wanted him the most, laving slowly, deliberately above, around, below her sweet spot.

Her frustrated moan echoed through the room. Her legs twined around his back, trying to position him where she wanted him.

He smiled against her thigh, then nipped her skin. Her surprised squeak filled his ears. "Patience, *mon amante*."

The scent of her arousal filled him with a ferocious compulsion to rise above her and plunge deep into her slick sleeve. Soon, he promised himself. The tendons of her wrists flexed and her pulse fluttered wildly beneath his fingertips. He relented and released her. Immediately one of her hands fisted the sheets. The other threaded through the hair at his nape, increasing his urgency.

He finally gave her swollen bud the attention she craved. Within moments her breath caught, her muscles tensed and she stilled, then orgasm overtook her. He rode out the undulations of her body, each one shooting an arrow of need straight to his groin.

She cupped his jaw and tugged upward. Normally he would have plied her over and over until she was boneless, but her extra boldness tonight had derailed his usual self-discipline.

He slowly ascended her body, dragging his overheated flesh against her damp skin. He poised above her and then remembered. A condom. *Merde.* He had not unpacked the box from his shaving kit which was in the bathroom. And Megan was here. Warm, wet and waiting.

Braced above her on straight arms he debated his options with what little cognizance he had remaining. Did he really need protection? They were both healthy. And she was already pregnant with his child.

He had never had unprotected sex. Never. But to share such intimacy with Megan seemed right. The possibility of sliding inside her unsheathed and experiencing every inch of her against every inch of him ignited a fire at the base of his spine.

Before he could have second thoughts he thrust into her. Her surprise-widened gaze met his. She, too, realized the significance of his actions. And then the hot, slick glove of her body surrounded him and all he could do was feel.

The absolute eroticism of being this close to her without barriers nearly overwhelmed him. He battled his body's demand to ride her hard and fast to the quickest climax of his adult life. He wanted to go slowly, to relish every moment until he could not last another second. But that outcome seemed doomed to failure.

As if she sensed his turmoil, she smiled. The sultry, sexy welcoming curve of her lips exacerbated his unraveling response. She thumbed the hypersensitive spot beneath his ear that never failed to arouse him, massaged his shoulders, then her palms descended ever so slowly across his pecs to flick his nipples. Jolts of intense pleasure surged through him. She caressed his ribs and abdomen. His muscles contracted like ripples of applause in the wake of her touch. Her short nails dug into his buttocks, pulling him deeper and fully seating him in her molten center. And then she squeezed him with her feminine muscles.

A groan he could not contain rocketed from his chest. The intensity of the sensations bombarding him went far beyond anything he had ever experienced. She had annihilated his willpower and pushed him past the line of no return. Animal instinct took over and his hunger blazed out of control. He withdrew, then plunged in again. For the first time in his life, he could not slow the pistoning of his hips, the wild race of his heart, the rapid cadence of his breaths.

Pending release built inside him like the pressure from an unvented boiler, then his climax exploded, pulsing over and over with white-hot bursts of heat. Passion roared up his throat and his hoarse groan drowned out the hammering beat of his heart.

Every muscle in his body quaked in the aftermath and his strength drained. His elbows buckled. He managed to land beside Megan instead of crushing her, but it was a near miss. The combination of their fluids as he slipped from her body seemed more intimate than anything he had shared with her—with anyone—in his life.

He lay beside her, fighting to fill his lungs and trying to regain his senses. Without the need to dispose of a condom he had no reason to leave her embrace—a good thing because he could not move. He had never been more sated in his life. Not one cell had been left wanting.

He drifted into a hazy presleep realm with a smile on his face and a sense of supreme satisfaction unraveling his thoughts. He realized this was the postsex total relaxation that other men talked about and he had never experienced. He'd come close, but this... *Ahh*. It felt good. Beyond good.

Megan nudged him from his euphoria by pulling her arm from beneath him. Then she leaned over him and brushed her lips across his. "Good night, Xavier."

His lids were too heavy to open, his thoughts too tangled to question her odd tone. "Good night, *mon amante*."

The mattress rocked. He felt a chill where her body had been and forced his eyes open just in time to see her shrugging on her robe and heading for the door.

The bedroom door, not the bathroom door.

The fog in his brain dissipated. He rolled up on his elbow.

"Where are you going?" His voice sounded hoarse, raspy.

"Back to my room. Sleep well." The connecting door closed behind her. Then the lock clicked, knocking him from his blissful state. He sat up in bed scowling at the closed *and locked* door.

Megan had left him. Women did not leave him. He left

them after the required amount of the required postcoital cuddling.

The shoe was on the other foot. And it was not at all comfortable.

About John the required amount of the neutral powdered conckine.

The state proved unacceptable. And it was typical of everybody else.

Six

Megan entered the sponsors-and-owners breakfast determined to make more useful American connections. If plan C came into play she'd have to find U.S. sponsors. And while she wasn't encouraging plan C, she wasn't going to miss this opportunity to cover her bases.

But the main reason she'd come was that being in this tent full of influential people gave her a legitimate reason to dodge an intimate meal with Xavier. And it would be the last place he'd look for her. After last night, she was on shaky ground and needed time to regroup.

Even at this early hour, affluent, well-dressed patrons packed the tent. She glanced at her khaki slacks and oxford-cloth blouse and grimaced. She should have spiffed herself up a bit. Too late now. She wasn't going back to that suite.

The temporary hardwood floor laid for the event tapped under her boot heels as she walked past the linen-draped tables decorated with beautiful floral arrangements. She nodded to a few familiar faces—people she'd competed against as a teen before leaving for Europe—but kept moving, searching the crowd for a target.

At the head of the buffet line, she declined a mimosa and accepted a crystal goblet filled with orange juice instead and moved toward the food, intent on ordering a custom-made omelet and snagging an advantageous seat at one of the tables.

She spotted a rock star and his equestrian daughter, a couple of actresses and their jodhpur-clad children and then finally a potential sponsor across the room, someone who had a long history with Sutherland Farm's stock. All she had to do was grab her food and get there before someone else claimed the seat beside him.

"Megan!" a familiar and unwelcome voice called from behind her making her groan silently. She fought the urge to pretend she hadn't heard and take off in the opposite direction. Instead she held her ground, forced a smile and faced one of her least favorite people.

"Good morning, Priscilla."

The catty gossip had been gunning for Megan in the ring for years. The fact that Megan always beat Prissy James in the jump-offs only upped the antagonism between them. But that was because Megan never caved under pressure. Prissy did. Every time. And Priss was a sore loser.

"So this is where you ran to. We've all been wondering where you'd gone to hide after Xavier's engagement announcement made the papers."

Megan's hackles rose. The accusation might be accurate, but that didn't mean she liked it any more than she enjoyed learning she was the topic of backstabbing gossip. Once her pregnancy became common knowledge the talk would only worsen.

"I'm not hiding. I'm working as a trainer for Sutherland

Farm and the timing of my job change was purely coincidental."

That was her story and she was sticking to it.

"You called your clients and bailed on the same day the engagement announcement ran in the papers."

"Like I said, the timing was a fluke. And I didn't bail on my clients. I helped all of them, including Xavier, find replacement riders for their horses. I came home because my cousin is getting married. I wanted to help her plan her wedding."

"Your cousin?" Clear disbelief hiked the woman's eyebrows.

"Hannah Sutherland. You've met her. She's a breeder and the only family I have."

"Not counting your uncle. But then you two don't get along, do you?"

Evil witch. Flinging the juice in her face would be so satisfying, but Megan wasn't the type to let a competitor get under her skin or in her head. "My uncle and I have had our share of disagreements, but he's retired now and no longer living on the farm."

"Well, you can't say I didn't warn you about Xavier's short attention span. Although I think you lasted longer than most of his women. His record was four months. And you were together how long…?"

Megan ignored the question. "What brings you to Lexington? I'm sure you didn't fly all the way across the Atlantic to check up on me."

Prissy's lips curled downward. "Didn't you hear? I'm selling my horse. He just can't place high enough."

She'd watched Priss and her horse often enough to know the horse wasn't the problem. "No, I hadn't heard."

"So I'm looking for a new mount—one who has championship qualities."

Priss was the type to blame the horse rather than accept responsibility for errors she made. But it wasn't Megan's place to say so. "I wish you luck in your search."

"Who are you riding today?"

"I'm not."

Those feline eyes searched Megan's face then her body looking for clues. "Really? Any reason?"

None that she'd share. "Just taking a break. After ten years, I deserve one, and the wedding prep is pretty time consuming. If you remember, Hannah doesn't have a mom around to help."

"Have you talked to Xavier since you split? He's left France."

How could she end this inane conversation? It wasn't going to get any better. And darn it. Someone had snagged the seat beside her potential sponsor. "I'm here with Xavier this weekend. He's leased a local farm and I'm working with his horses."

"Oh? Is he going to set you up stateside and keep his wife in France?"

Great. Prissy had her version of the truth and she'd spread it to anyone who'd listen to her poison unless Megan could convince her otherwise. "Don't be ridiculous. I'm here as his trainer as he tests the American circuit and some up-and-coming riders. One of the guys I'm coaching is riding Xavier's horses and mine this weekend."

The cat's gaze turned speculative. "You're not riding at all? Are you injured or…something?"

If Prissy figured out the secret it might as well be broadcast by the Associated Press. "Nope. I'm getting a little R&R."

"Oh, really?" Another I-don't-believe-you jab.

Be nice, Megs. But she couldn't help it. She had to knock

the witch off the throne she'd put herself on. So what if it meant helping an adversary?

"Priss, because we're not competing against each other I'm going to give you a piece of helpful advice. Your losses are your fault. Not your mount's. And it doesn't matter whether you ride a new horse or your current one, you're going to get the same result until *you* change.

"You ride well in the competitions, but you tense up in every jump-off. And you blow it. You squeeze your legs too tight and hold your reins in a death grip. *You* are unconsciously telling Jezebel to take an extra half-stride between each jump. That's why you knock down rails. Not because your horse makes a mistake. But because *you* do.

"And now, if you'll excuse me, I only have a few minutes to grab breakfast before I head to the practice ring."

She pivoted away from Priss's reddening face, grabbed a plate and silverware and marched down the buffet line. She would not run. Running would only confirm the nasty woman's words. Instead Megan gritted a smile and pushed herself to do exactly what she'd come here to do. Eat and make connections. She might have missed her opportunity with one sponsor, but she'd find others.

The chef piled her plate with a grilled asparagus, prosciutto and Swiss cheese omelet and a side of spicy sausage—two items that would have made her salivate ten minutes ago. But her appetite had fled with the knowledge that her life was being dissected by her old acquaintances. Anything she did even on this side of the ocean would be news until a hotter topic or juicier scandal came along.

Plan C wasn't an option if she wanted to hold her head up in the equestrian community.

Breakfast hadn't improved Megan's mood. Reconnecting with undemanding former acquaintances had given her

mind time to wander. She had analyzed the data and the
players involved in her situation and come up with one
inescapable conclusion.

Her current predicament was her fault.

She gave herself a mental kick in the pants as she
watched Tim circle the practice ring on Rocky Start, her
junior horse. She had convinced herself over the years that
she was too smart to fall in love. She was paying for her
cockiness now.

She'd never looked for a soul mate because she hadn't
planned to have a family of her own. Instead she'd focused
on her career and vowed not to let anyone who might tie
her down or demand she take time away from her horses
get too close. She'd learned the hard way that loved ones
could be snatched away instantly and without warning.

The few-and-far-between relationships she'd had before
Xavier had been of the friends-with-benefits variety. They
had been satisfying enough without rockets or fireworks,
and they had served their intended purpose—physical relief
with someone whose company she enjoyed, someone she
liked and respected.

When she'd met Xavier she'd expected to follow the same
good-while-it-lasts model. And it had started that way—
just fun and passion. *Lots* of passion. Their relationship had
been perfect until he'd popped her self-protective bubble
by buying the cottage for her. And then he'd wormed his
way deeper into her heart when he'd helped her decorate
it.

"Nesting" with him had given her the first home she'd
had since her parents' and brother's deaths. That, she decided, was what had made her want him for keeps and what
had led her to this point.

And when she'd plotted out crazy plan B she'd fooled
herself into believing she could keep her heart insulated

while sleeping with him. But every time she built a wall Xavier found a way to knock it down. Last night, when she'd been fighting for detachment, he'd shattered her defenses by not wearing protection. One simple omission, the lack of a physical barrier between them, had made the act of sex even more intimate.

She kept reminding herself that he'd emptied his seed deep inside her only because he had nothing to lose. She was already pregnant. Otherwise it never would have happened. Not intentionally.

How long would it take him to realize they shared so much more than potent chemistry? Would he ever? Or was she fighting a losing battle?

Quitters never win.

As her cousin had pointed out, Megan wasn't a quitter. Her never-give-up motto in the ring contributed in a large way to her success. As Hannah had advised, Megan needed to apply that same dedication to her relationship with Xavier.

She couldn't give up on this—her most important battle to date. If Xavier wanted to pretend their relationship was still only about sex, then she would continue to give him exactly that. Only sex, no matter how much it hurt to treat the magic they made each time they touched as though it were as trivial as scratching an itch.

But no doubt about it—plan B sucked. And it hurt. Like getting thrown and having the wind knocked out of her.

Leaving his bed last night with her heart still racing, her body still damp and her muscles deliciously relaxed had been one of the hardest things she'd ever done. She wasn't sure how long she could keep it up without it destroying her.

"Did you sleep well in your solitary bed, *chérie?*" Xavier's hard voice immediately behind her startled her.

He wouldn't have to ask if she'd slept well if he knew how much makeup it had taken to cover the dark circles beneath her eyes. Faking a calm expression and a smile that in no way reflected her inner turmoil, she turned away from the ring, Rocky Start and Tim.

"I always sleep like the dead after sex. You?"

"I would have preferred you to stay." She considered the admission a tiny victory—even though he looked as if he'd swallowed something bitter as he said it. "You missed breakfast and you did not answer when I knocked on your door."

His underlying anger may or may not be a good thing. "You said I should act like an owner. So I did. I left early and grabbed breakfast in the tent with a few of the other owners, then I helped Tim get my horses ready."

"That is the groom's job."

"Only if you can afford one."

He frowned. "Mine are at your disposal."

"For how long, Xavier?" She had to make him realize that nothing was going to be the same. "You've spoiled me by letting me share your staff. I need to get used to taking care of my own horses again. I'm out of practice."

The lines in his brow deepened. "That is not necessary."

"I disagree. When you and your horses return to Europe—and you will—I'll be here. On my own." Unless she won this fight and convinced him to give her the home and family she had never dreamed of but now desperately craved.

The overhead speaker announced Tim's class and Megan's adrenaline instantly kicked in. This would normally be her moment to shine, her time to prove to the world—and her uncle—that Megan Sutherland was more than some hack rider or *that woman's* child. It would also be the moment she leaned down from the saddle for Xavier's good-luck kiss before she rode toward the arena.

But not today.

Today she had to put aside her disappointment that there would be no kiss, and she'd have to reel in her competitive urges, don her new supportive instructor hat and let someone else go for the glory. None of it was going to be easy.

The possibility of being forced to give up this life permanently made her stomach cramp with nerves she'd never experienced when riding. Riding was all she knew. She didn't have a college degree to fall back on since she'd left her uncle's home the day after graduating high school.

Xavier moved closer, his body heat and scent enfolded her and the urge to lean into his embrace was as involuntary as the need to take her next breath. "Are you also going to refuse to join me in the front-row box seats which I have reserved?"

"No. I'll join you." She waved Tim over. He trotted Rocky to the rail and stopped. His tension was clear in his pale face. Megan petted Rocky's strong neck and ached to be on the other side of the fence. It was so hard to let someone else ride her horses—especially since Tim didn't seem to thrive on the competition the way she did.

"Tim, remember this is just an opportunity to get your feet wet at a bigger show against stiffer competition. You have nothing to lose. You're not out there to win. If you place, great, but that's not your goal today. Your goal is to do your best and get as clean a round as you can. Focus on the basics. Remember what we talked about when we walked the course this morning. Keep your eyes on the top rail and you'll be fine."

Tim gulped and nodded. "I'll try, Megan. I don't want to let you down."

"This isn't about me. This is about you showing yourself

what you can do. You have the ability and a good mount. All you need is practice. Nobody's expecting perfection. Least of all me." She gave him two thumbs-up.

Looking only slightly less tense, he nodded and turned toward the show ring behind the other equestrians. Rocky, eager as always to get to the course, had to be reined in. Megan stared after them, wishing, yearning to be in that saddle.

"Giving him five new mounts in a show of this caliber is too much too soon for him."

"He will learn."

"Not if you sour him on riding first."

"If that happens then he was not born to be a competitor."

Xavier grasped her elbow and steered her toward the stands. He easily carved a path through the crowd. The attendee's apparel ranged from designer to denim with some of the women wearing wide-brimmed hats worthy of the Queen Mother or Kentucky Derby. Megan's clothes fell somewhere in the middle. Translation—nothing special. Just like her.

As promised, Xavier led her to front-row seats, center ring—the best vantage point in the house. No surprise since Xavier never did anything by half-measure even on short notice. But getting these seats couldn't have been easy or inexpensive.

Megan perched on the edge of her chair, trying to acclimate herself to being on the wrong side of the fence. She wasn't used to being surrounded by people, conversation, food and movement. Riding? Yes. Standing ringside and assessing her competition? Absolutely. But sitting still in the stands? Hard to do when her heart pounded faster than the horse and rider cantering past her toward the starting line.

She could smell the arena dirt, the flowers that decorated

some of the jumps and the chlorine in the water filling the Liverpools. All normal. But the overpowering perfume of the lady to her left, the bourbon stench from the man on Xavier's right were out of place in her mind. The last two hammered home that this wasn't where she belonged or where she wanted to be. Xavier took her hand in his, his thumb sweeping back and forth across her palm, yet another distraction, one that agitated a beehive in her belly.

The rider approached the first jump. Megan caught herself counting strides, leaning forward and putting her weight on the balls of her feet as if she were in the saddle. Embarrassed, she abruptly sat back and shot a quick glance at Xavier. She caught him watching her instead of the horse and rider.

Satisfaction glimmered in his eyes. *Satisfaction?* The emotion seemed out of place. He gave her fingers a squeeze. "You miss the competition."

Nothing like stating the obvious. But she wouldn't give him the pleasure or ammunition of agreeing. "Observing from the sidelines provides an opportunity to study the riders and horses I'll face next year when I return to competition."

As soon as she said the words, another thought registered. She could also use her time to identify the riders with young children—few though they may be—and then she could approach them to see if any of them might be interested in sharing a nanny while they were on the road during the show season.

She'd work something else out for Monday through Wednesday when she was at the farm. Maybe Nellie, the Sutherland Farm housekeeper who'd all but raised Megan and Hannah after their mothers' deaths, would be interested in watching the baby part-time.

Hold that thought. Megan could subtly ask questions and

gather information as long as she didn't reveal why. She wasn't ready to have the news of her condition traveling the gossip grapevine fast on the heels of Xavier's engagement announcement and her relocation—especially not after Prissy's revelations this morning. People would talk about his past lover and his future wife and might rightly connect the dots of her baby's paternity.

Any fiancée worthy of the title would—*should*—come winging across the ocean to defend her turf if she heard her husband-to-be had a baby on the way with another woman.

Megan had a better chance of convincing Xavier to break his engagement if his beautiful, blonde, perfect fiancée wasn't around to muddy the waters.

The sound of a rail clattering down and the heat of Xavier's rock-solid thigh beneath their joined hands shocked Megan with the realization that she hadn't been paying attention. She tugged her hand from Xavier's and forced herself to concentrate on the horse and rider completing the course.

She had to get her head back in the game and weigh the odds of Tim and Rocky besting this entry. There was so much to learn from sitting in the stands. All she had to do was keep the big French distraction beside her from derailing her concentration.

She managed to maintain her focus through the next two riders, then the announcer called out Tim's name and Rocky Start. Megan's heart bounded wildly. Funny how much more nervous she was watching her horse than riding him. She leaned forward, clutching the edge of her seat as Rocky and his rider entered the arena and cantered toward the beginning of the course. Tim looked as nervous as she felt when he paused then backed Rocky two steps. He nodded to the judges, waiting for permission to begin. The gelding pranced uneasily in place, obviously picking up Tim's agitation. A lump rose in Megan's throat.

And then horse and rider were off. Xavier's palm curved over Megan's shoulder. He leaned forward until his breath teased the hair by her ear and she shivered, darn it, her reaction to him one that she couldn't turn off.

"Say the word, *mon amante,* and you can return to competition next season unencumbered."

She glared at him, missing Rocky's approach to the first oxer. Xavier was offering her the simplest solution. Give up her baby and her life could return to "normal." But she wasn't interested in her old version of normal anymore, and she'd never been the type to take shortcuts or the easy way out. She wasn't going to start now.

Then she noticed the cunning, watchful expression in his eyes and a lightbulb of understanding switched on. The devil was using her strategy against her. *He* was trying to show *her* what she'd be missing if she continued on her current path.

The nerve of him. That's why he'd paid the exorbitant entry fees for her horses, reserved a five-star hotel room, bought the designer apparel for her and ordered her favorite foods. It had nothing to do with her mattering to him and everything to do with him trying to manipulate her into giving him what he wanted. Her baby.

Well, he'd have to be smarter than that if he planned to get the best of her. She was in it to win it. Her life and her child's depended on her coming out on top.

Second place was, after all, the first loser.

Tonight would be different, Megan vowed as she pushed away from their late-night, postshow feast.

Tonight she wouldn't lose control or forget her objective.

Tonight she would bring Xavier to his knees—sexually speaking—but keep her emotional distance.

And then maybe leaving him all warm and sated in his bed wouldn't hurt so much.

She rose, stepped away from the table and slowly undid the side zip of the dress he'd given her for tonight's event, this one a rich ruby-red and strapless. The garment slid to the floor, leaving her in the sexy red bustier bra and panties and beaded scarlet do-me heels.

Without taking his eyes from her, Xavier leaned back in his chair and reached for his tie, loosening the knot and sliding the silk free in a slithering swish. He looped the end of the tie around the middle. Odd. And then she realized he was tying a slipknot. Why?

"You're going to wrinkle the silk."

"The cleaner will take care of it." He repeated the procedure on the opposite end of the fabric and stood, holding the double loops in one hand. Slowly. Deliberately. He stalked in her direction, like a tiger preparing to pounce.

Her heart pumped wildly. They had never played games of restraint. Was that his goal? Gulping, she backed one step, then two. "What are you doing?"

"Preparing to pleasure you."

She turned and headed toward his room. He caught her fingers, pulled her close and twirled her the way he had on the dance floor at tonight's cocktail party.

The silk tie skimmed down her spine, cool and smooth against her bare skin. It settled at her waist. A loop encircled one wrist, then the second loop captured the other, tethering her hands by her sides. Adrenaline rushed through her system caused not by fear, but excitement. "Xavier—"

"Do you trust me, Megan?" His dark green gaze probed hers.

"Of course I do, but I—"

His mouth covered hers. The kiss was deep and seductive, potent and lethal to her vow to remain detached. His lips plied her mouth and their tongues tangled. Warm palms buffed her ribs, waist and hips then cupped her bottom and pressed her closer.

She tried to free her hands to touch him, but she couldn't. Pulling only tightened the restraints. The loops weren't painful and weren't cutting off circulation. But they might if she continued to fight them.

She had to get control of this situation. Planting a stiletto in the carpet, she attempted to steer him toward his bedroom—hard to do without hands. When the shoulder nudges failed, she shuffled toward the sitting room sofa, and when that didn't work, the table—any horizontal surface where she could leave him after the sex. Anywhere that wasn't her bed where she would retreat to lick her wounds in solitude later.

She felt him smile against her mouth, and then he bent and scooped her into his arms. She couldn't wrap her arms around his neck to hold on and therefore didn't dare struggle in case he dropped her.

He carried her into her bedroom and deposited her on her feet beside the turned-back bed. This wasn't going at all the way she'd planned.

"The condoms are in your room," she protested. "Let's go there."

"We don't need them. I enjoyed being inside you last night with nothing between us."

A swoop of desire rocked her belly. "Untie me and let me touch you."

"Later." His mouth steamed the side of her neck a split second before his teeth lightly grazed her skin just below her ear.

She gasped then when he released her bra and cradled

her breasts, thumbing the tips into tight knots that tangled her insides even more. She moaned involuntarily.

"Xavier, I need to touch you, too."

"You are touching me." He cupped her elbows and shifted his torso against hers. The placket of his shirt gently abraded her taut nipples and his cold belt buckle pressed her stomach—a sharp contrast to the hot length of his arousal below. He shoved his hands into her panties, his palms blazing against her cool buttocks as he cupped and caressed her, then he eased the lacy garment down her legs. It pooled at her ankles, leaving both her wrists and ankles captive. She kicked the garment away, and in the process, her shoes.

His hands skimmed, brushed, stroked and plucked, sweeping away her love-him-and-leave-him strategy with effortless ease. Damn him. Her muscles quivered and hunger welled within her.

Focus. Remember this is about sex. That's all he thinks he wants. And that's all you're going to give him. This is not about the way he gets into your head or the way he finds every magical erogenous spot on your body and plies it until you want to beg him to relieve your pent-up desire.

But damn, he does it so well.

He lifted her and laid her on the bed. The weight of her body sank into the plush mattress, pulling the slack from the tie under her and truly anchoring her hands to her sides. She couldn't lift her fists from the bed.

He leaned over her, still fully dressed, and took her mouth again, hard and fast, then moved on to her neck, her ears. He inched ever so slowly to her breasts, tormenting her with his soft lips, his hot tongue, and then her personal weakness—his raspy chin.

Hurry. Hurry. Hurry. She silently pleaded with him to get this over with before she cracked. But he lingered, sipping, laving, nibbling gently and then just rough enough to send a sharp arrow of hunger shooting through her. Her toes and fingers curled.

Maintaining her mental distance was the only way to get through tonight without losing another chunk of her soul. Squeezing her eyes shut, she tried to recall the jumps on this afternoon's course, tried to replay Tim's approach to the ones he'd knocked down and figure out where he'd gone wrong. The lead changes, the strides, the horse drifting to one side or another.

A rattling sound distracted her from her mental movie. Before she could identify it, shocking cold coated her left nipple. Her body jerked and her eyes flew open. "Wh-what is that?"

But she knew. Ice. Xavier circled her aureole with the freezing cube, then replaced it with his scalding hot mouth. A guttural sound rumbled up her throat. One of surprise. One of enthusiastic approval. One of desire more potent than anything she'd experienced previously. She couldn't have held back the sound if she tried. They had never played this game before, either. And ohmigod she liked it.

He repeated the icy/hot process on the opposite breast and she shuddered. So good.

Focus, Megan. Focus.

On what? her distracted brain asked.

On the slow glide of the ice cube between her breasts and then down her midline. On the cold circle he drew around her navel. On the melting rivulets running down her sides. On the icy drip trickling over her hottest spot.

Her entire body went rigid. Then his mouth replaced the ice, his oh-so-talented *hot* mouth. Her hands clutched the sheets. Climax bunched inside her, twisting, tightening, building. She fought it. She couldn't let him win. And then, despite her struggle, it broke free, undulating through her in uncontrollable spasms of ecstasy.

"Do you wish me to stop, *mon amante?*"

"No. Please don't. Oh, Xavier. I need you inside me."

A slow smile curved his lips. "Not yet. But soon."

He reached toward the ice bucket on the bedside table and extracted another cube.

And Megan groaned in defeat. Any strategy she'd had to keep her emotional distance from him tonight had melted faster than the ice with which he'd tormented her. She'd try again tomorrow. Because tonight he'd annihilated her strategy.

Home at last.

Megan dropped her suitcase inside the cottage foyer Sunday evening and sagged against the closed door. Every muscle in her body whimpered with exhaustion.

After two nights of making love with Xavier and three days of pretending it—*he*—didn't matter, all she wanted was to crawl into a hole and pull the dirt in on top of her. Especially after last night when he'd totally defeated her with orgasm after orgasm.

He'd broken her. Made her beg. And afterward he'd held her. And she'd cried in his arms. Cried, damn it. She didn't think he'd noticed. But she knew. That's what mattered. She'd silently cried for what they'd had. And what they'd lost. Then he'd slept in her bed, destroying her intention of tending her wounds in private.

Her stomach growled, but she had no energy to prepare a meal. For the baby's sake she would force down a banana and a glass of milk, but what she truly craved was a hot shower and bed. She headed toward the bathroom. A knock on the front door stopped her short of her goal. Groaning, she considered ignoring it. But she hadn't turned the lock.

If it was Xavier, he'd just barge in. At least if she answered, she stood a chance of keeping him outside.

Pasting a smile on her face, she backtracked and opened the door. Hannah stood on the front mat, her arms loaded. "Whoa, that's your I'll-be-nice-to-you-even-if-it-kills-me smile. What's wrong?"

Her cousin read her too well. Most people fell for the mask. Megan's tense muscles uncoiled. "I'm just tired."

"I brought some of Nellie's Cajun fettuccini Alfredo. Does bringing dinner buy me entry?" She offered a casserole dish.

Megan's mouth watered as she took it. For Nellie's cooking she'd delay her shower. "You know it. Lock the door behind you."

"Oookay." The way she stretched the word revealed Hannah knew Megan never locked her doors, but then growing up in the country meant they hadn't needed to. Hannah dropped the oversize clothing bag she had draped over her arm on a chair along with a large shopping bag and followed Megan to the kitchen. "How was your weekend?"

Megan set the dish on the table, grateful she'd removed her sticky notes from the fridge. "None of the horses placed, but Tim did a great job considering it was his first big show. He didn't crack under the pressure. He only had eight faults on Apollo and—"

"I wasn't asking about the horses or Tim, Megs."

Megan hid a grimace behind the open cabinet door. "Are you joining me?"

"Absolutely. Wyatt's out of town and Nellie has her book club meeting tonight, so it's just us girls." Hannah peeled back the foil covering their dinner and the delicious aroma made Megan's stomach rumble with anticipation. "Ohmigod, this smells heavenly. How was your time with Xavier?"

"Are you trying to kill my appetite? Nellie's feelings will be hurt if there are leftovers." She carried the plates and utensils to the table.

"She'll never know. I'll leave the evidence here. Spill it."

Megan didn't want to worry Hannah, but her cousin could be stubborn when she set her mind to something, and she'd obviously decided she couldn't live without the details of Megan's weekend.

"We're sleeping together."

"Why doesn't that sound like good news?"

"Because it isn't. Exactly. He thinks our relationship is all about the sex. I decided the only way to prove he's wrong is by giving him sex and only sex. No cuddles. No shared breakfasts in bed. No talking over coffee or nightcaps. I'll withhold everything that isn't directly related to physical gratification."

Hannah's brow pleated and worry darkened her eyes. "That's…an unusual strategy. I know I suggested you show him what you could give him that his fiancée can't, but…I don't know about this, Megan. It could backfire in a big way."

As it had last night. She'd never been more sexually sated in her life, nor more emotionally empty than after that marathon session.

"I'm aware of the risks, but it's the best approach I could come up with. It'll work. If not, like you said, what do I have to lose?" If she had any luck at all, Hannah would fall for her blasé tone. She scooped a portion of pasta onto her plate and picked up her fork, hoping to end the conversation. "So…enough talk. Let's eat. There's a hot shower waiting with my name on it."

Hannah paused with her fork just shy of her mouth.

"Well…after we're done I have another favor to ask. If you're up for it."

Uh-oh. At the moment solitude was the only thing that appealed. "What?"

"I brought my mother's wedding dress with me. I was hoping to try it on and get your opinion."

Megan's heart twinged a little. She couldn't be happier for Hannah, but it hurt to know that unless things changed she would never be trying on wedding dresses. However, she refused to be a killjoy. She reached across the table and squeezed Hannah's hand. "I would love to see you in your mother's dress. I remember how much we used to beg to play dress-up in it."

Hannah's smile was a little sad. "And she always said, 'Your day will come.' And now it has."

They made quick work of dinner, staying away from the topic of Xavier, thank heaven, then returned to the den. Hannah unzipped the long garment bag and extracted the lavish, full-skirted lace gown.

Megan's breath caught. She stroked her hand over the delicate fabric. "There's something special about older wedding gowns that today's modern mass-produced ones just don't have."

"I agree." Hannah looked a little misty-eyed. "And I can't imagine wearing anything else."

Even if Xavier came to his senses, there would be no vintage gown for Megan. Her mother hadn't had a wedding dress. Because her paternal grandparents had disapproved of their younger son's relationship with a lowly cocktail waitress, her mom and dad had eloped and returned home with the legalities a done deal. Her father's family—especially Uncle Luthor—had never forgiven them.

Hannah's mother had been the only family member who hadn't made Megan and her mom feel like outcasts. In fact, she'd insisted Megan join Hannah's riding lessons and had spent hours coaching the girls herself. Hannah's mom had claimed helping Megan was the least she could do since Megan's father had introduced her to her husband.

Hannah grabbed Megan's hand. "Megs, I want you to be my maid of honor."

Megan's heart took another roller-coaster plunge. "Are you sure? I mean I'll be…" She mimed a bulging belly.

"Of course I'm sure. There's no one more important to me. Besides, there are no rules prohibiting pregnant bridesmaids. Even if there were, I'd break 'em."

"Then I'd be honored."

"That means helping me pick out the announcements and stuff. It won't be all fun and bachelorette parties."

"I can handle it." Tears threatened to choke her. Darn these pregnancy hormones. "Now, stop talking and try on this dress. I can't wait to see you in it."

Hannah grinned and shed her clothing then reached for the gown. Megan helped her get the garment over her head.

"Turn around. Let me do the buttons." She slipped the satin-covered buttons through the loops wishing their mothers could have been here for this, but as with most of their milestones she and Hannah had only had each other. "Done."

Hannah swept her hands over the full skirt and twirled so that it belled around her.

"Gorgeous. You look like a princess."

"Y'think? I probably won't wear Mom's long veil because we'd like to get married at the boathouse and I'm afraid it might snag on the dock."

"The boathouse is kinda small—not much room for guests."

"Yes, but it has special meaning."

"Because that's where you and your mom always went to celebrate every new beginning and every ending?"

A secret smile danced across Hannah's lips. "Among other things. It's the place where Wyatt and I first made lo—"

Megan stuck her fingers in her ears. "La la la. I don't want to know." Then, all kidding aside, she looked at the dress and at Hannah's radiant face. "It's perfect. It doesn't even need to be altered to fit you."

"Do you really think so?"

"I do."

"Wyatt and I want a small, intimate ceremony with just my dad, Nellie, Wyatt's stepfather and you as witnesses. Then we'll have a grand reception on the lawn for the Sutherland Farm employees and any others on the must-invite list. If we have it here, any staff members who are scheduled to work that Saturday can slip in for a bit. That means the attire for the reception will be casual. And if it rains we can set up in the indoor riding arena."

"It sounds wonderful."

"Now for your bridesmaid dress, what color do you think you'd—"

A knock on the front door interrupted—a firm, no-nonsense pounding that told Megan who was on the other side even before the knob rattled.

Megan's muscles tensed. "Thank heaven you locked the door."

"Xavier?"

Megan nodded.

"Sweetie, my car is outside and every light in the house is on. Even with the curtains closed, he'll know we're here. You can't run away from this. You're going to have to let him in. But I have your back, okay? And we'll get rid of him fast. We have a wedding to plan."

Megan's heart slid to her boots. She was so not ready to face Xavier again—especially not now when in all likelihood his bride-to-be was at home choosing a wedding dress of her own.

The weekend had been less than satisfactory. Xavier fumed silently as he stood on Megan's porch. He had expected the horse show to make her realize that she could not keep the child and compete.

Rather than yearning for the ring, she had used the time she usually spent focused on him or her mounts talking to equestrians with small children. She had not mentioned her pregnancy to anyone in his presence, but had instead explored the logistics of having a nanny.

She was not going to relinquish their baby easily. He should admire her for that. But that meant he had to employ an alternative strategy—one that would complicate his life.

He pounded on the door again, and when she didn't answer immediately, he grasped the knob. It did not turn. The fact that she had chosen to heed his advice and start locking her door now that he needed to speak to her magnified his irritation.

He heard footsteps inside, then the door opened a few inches. Megan's unwelcoming face appeared in the breach. "I'm busy here, Xavier. What do you want?"

Not the reception he had anticipated. Particularly after last night's combustive sex. But he would not be sent away like an annoying child. He flattened his palm on the wood and pushed his way into the foyer. Yes, he was being obnoxious, but Megan was playing games. Games he did not like. And she was forcing him to compromise— something he liked even less.

"You left while I was on the phone."

"There was no reason to stay, and I wanted to get home and have my shower."

"We could have showered together. You know how much you enjoy my touch when I wash your—"

"Ahem." The sound of a feminine voice clearing snatched his attention to the den. Megan's cousin stood in the adjoining room. Wearing a wedding dress. "Hello, Xavier."

The words did not sound hospitable in the least.

"Good evening, Hannah." He turned a questioning glance to Megan.

"Like I said, I'm busy."

"I will take you to dinner when you finish with…this." He indicated the dress with a flick of his wrist.

"I've eaten."

She would not dismiss him so easily. "I must speak to you. Tonight. I will wait." He entered the den and planted himself on the sofa.

Megan remained in the foyer with her hand on the doorknob. "Xavier—"

"It's okay, Megan," her cousin interrupted in a singsong voice that did not bode well. "Xavier has a wedding of his own to plan, and it will do him good to suffer through our little exercise tonight. Men have absolutely no concept of how much work and planning it takes to pull together even the simplest of ceremonies."

The women exchanged a long look, which he could not decipher, then with an aggrieved expression, Megan swung the door closed. "If you insist on staying, you should know this could take a while."

He shrugged. "I have nowhere else to be tonight since I had anticipated spending it with you." He turned to the bride-to-be. "If it is so important that the man be involved why is your fiancé not here?"

"He's not supposed to see me in the dress, and he's letting Megan, Nellie and me arrange some of the small details since he swears all that matters is that the *right people* are taking the vows."

He accepted the dig in silence. The cousin had an ax to grind—one she would prefer to bury in his back, he suspected. "Wise of him to let the women handle the preparations."

He was only throwing fuel on the fire, and the reddening of Hannah's cheeks confirmed he had scored. But he did not mind riling Megan's cousin. He suspected Hannah had something to do with Megan's odd behavior of late.

Hannah shook her finger at him. "While you're partying at horse shows in the States, your fiancée is probably neck-deep in a hectic rush of ordering a custom-made designer gown, reserving the church and reception venue and engaging musicians, caterers and florists. The least you could do is go home to sample the wedding cake and reception food choices."

His idea of hell. "She will contact me if my opinion is required."

Hannah glared. He held her gaze until she looked away. "Help me change, Megs, and then we'll start on the other stuff." She scooped up a pile of clothing and headed for Megan's bedroom in a swish of ivory fabric.

This was the woman with whom Megan had spent her youth? The one she claimed was as close as a sister? Both had glossy dark hair and blue eyes, but there the similarities ceased. He marveled at the differences in temperament. Megan would not dare to be so ill-mannered. She had a comportment about her that was not only attractive, but it served her well on the Grand Prix circuit where connections and the opinions of others could be critically important. Favoritism, though officials denied its existence, was rampant in judging.

With one last irritated glance at him, Megan followed her cousin and closed the door.

Xavier tried to be patient while the women conducted whatever business they must in the adjoining bedroom. He could hear the hum of their voices but could not make out the words. In his mind he saw the bed in the room they occupied, the one he and Megan had shared—and would again tonight if he had his way.

His body reacted predictably with a hot flush of desire and anticipation, and when he recalled last night's encounter he only became hotter. Friday night, Megan had held back, then she had left him even before the sweat dried on his skin. Saturday night, he had made certain she could neither hold back nor leave him. If she wanted to turn their physical relationship into some kind of competition, then he would win—as she had discovered to their mutual satisfaction. She had been too weak to even lift her head by the time he had finished with her last night.

He shoved to his feet and adjusted his suddenly tight clothing. But when she had finally fallen asleep and rolled away from him, the sheet she had clutched in her hand had been damp. Tears? He did not like the idea of Megan crying.

He pushed the uncomfortable thought aside and studied the portrait above the fireplace. The woman holding the reins of a horse bore an uncanny resemblance to Hannah. He turned to the multitude of photographs on the wall of horses and riders and searched for any of Megan. He found none.

Hannah's babble about Cecille's wedding plans had made him claustrophobic. The pomp and circumstance were only for the women. He did not care where the ceremony linking him to Cecille took place or what foods were served. The hows and wheres were irrelevant. The only item of importance was the reason *why* the wedding must take place.

The marriage would right the last of the wrongs his father had committed and the merger of two companies would take Parfums Alexandre to a level of success his father had never envisioned. And with Monsieur Debussey's pending retirement, Xavier would soon be CEO of the largest privately owned perfumerie in the world. With power came prestige. No one would be able to look down their nose at him again once he finalized this merger.

The bedroom door opened and the women returned, Hannah carrying the dress and looking antagonistic, Megan appearing resigned—an expression he had not seen on her face before today. She was usually the driven one, the one with a plan, a goal and a refusal to settle for less.

And she had once desired him with that ferocity of focus. But something had changed along with her pregnancy and her return home. She might claim it was his engagement but she had always known that one day they would part.

Physically he could still make her body sing as he'd proven repeatedly over the past two nights. But there had been a difference in her response this weekend that he could not fathom. The way she had slipped from his house earlier this evening when he was preoccupied with an urgent business call reinforced her eagerness to get away from him.

The idea that he might have crushed her tender feelings toward him bothered him—a ridiculous circumstance considering he had not asked for nor did he want an emotional attachment. To her or anyone else. Something he had very clearly spelled out in the beginning of their relationship.

Hannah tucked the wedding gown into a garment bag. Megan assisted her, stroking a hand over the fabric with a wistful expression that stabbed Xavier with another thought. Would Megan ever marry? If so, what kind of man would she choose?

The idea of her lying with someone else, bearing someone else's children disturbed him. But he could not ask her to stop living once their paths diverged.

Once the garment bag was zipped Hannah lifted a double-handled shopping bag. "You know how much I like photo albums and charts. Well, I've been busy. My head is full of ideas. I have pictures of potential bridesmaid dresses, sample invitations, a variety of menus and…all kinds of other stuff."

She unloaded one thick volume onto the coffee table, then a second. Megan shifted uneasily, glanced at Xavier, then held up a hand. "I'm sorry, Hannah. Can we do this another time?"

Hannah made a sympathetic moue at Megan, then glared at Xavier, shooting daggers through eyes so similar to her cousin's. But her eyes lacked the tenderness Megan's usually showed.

"I'll come back when you don't have an uninvited guest in the house." Hannah gathered her belongings and paused in front of Xavier. "I know where you live."

He managed not to laugh at the implied threat from a female as slight as Hannah.

Megan walked her cousin to the door and closed it behind her. Looking tired but resigned to his company, Megan parked her hands on her hips. "What do you want?"

"You did not enjoy the horse show."

"Not really. No. It was much too soon to ask Tim to compete against horses and riders of that caliber. That made the competition a bad experience for him and one he'll be reluctant to repeat. But I learned a lot."

"You learned that you do not like sitting in the audience."

"Among other things." She folded her arms, her face stubbornly set.

She was not going to give an inch. "I have found a way for you to have everything you desire—your career and our baby."

Her arms dropped and hope filled her eyes. "Really?"

"I will hire a nanny who will stay with *le bébé* year-round. Our child will reside with you in the States during the off-season and with me in France the remainder of the year."

He watched her closely, expecting her to gratefully accept his generous concession. But the militant expression overtaking her face could in no way be mistaken for gratitude.

Seven

"You're suggesting shared custody?" Megan supposed that was an improvement over Xavier wanting to buy the baby or take it away from her completely.

"*Oui*. That way we will both be able to spend time with our child."

Most women—those without her history—would probably jump at his offer. But joint custody wasn't even close to either of the outcomes she preferred—the three of them as a family or her as a single parent. She'd heard too many horror stories of children going overseas with their foreign parent only to become entangled in legal red tape and never return. She couldn't risk letting Xavier take their child out of the States.

"But that's not fair. You'd have him or her for the majority of the year and I'd get a lousy few months."

"Approximately."

She shook her head. "My child wouldn't even know me.

It would be better for the baby not to be torn between two parents, two cultures, two languages and two continents."

"How could it not be best for our child to have two involved parents?"

"Would you be involved, Xavier? You're the CEO of a large company. You work ten to twelve-hour days. How much time will you be able to devote to being a father? A child needs someone who will be there, someone who loves him or her and won't leave the parenting to nannies."

"You also intend to employ a nanny. And as you saw this weekend, there is little time for parenting on the circuit."

"Ah, yes, your plan. Don't think I didn't figure it out."

His eyes turned guarded. *"Pardon?"*

"I know you too well for that innocent expression to work on me. You were hoping to show me everything I'll give up if I choose to keep our baby. The competition, cocktail parties with the rich and famous, designer fashion, five-star hotels... But guess what? Your plan backfired.

"Each of those business icons we met is a potential sponsor to replace Parfums Alexandre when I start competing again. And I met at least three women who might be willing to share a nanny with me. The baby could accompany me to every show, and we'd never have to spend a night apart. You can't say the same."

"You are forgetting that my future wife will have a part in the child rearing."

"No, I'm not. But you are. Have you even told Cecille about our little surprise? How does she feel about being presented with a ready-made family and having a five-month-old waiting for her when she returns from her honeymoon?"

His flattening lips suggested he hadn't had that very important discussion. "She will adapt."

"Xavier, it's not about just what you want anymore.

It's about a little boy or girl who's going to need love—
unconditional, overflowing love. That's something I'm not
sure you're capable of giving. And you're assuming Cecille
will be happy to mother her husband's bastard."

The term repulsed her, but how else could she make
him see that not everyone would view the circumstances
of their baby's birth in a positive light?

He recoiled. Dark slashes of color swept his cheekbones
and fury burned in his eyes. She had never seen Xavier
this angry. Had she pushed too hard? Alarm and adrenaline
charged through her, kicking in her fight-or-flight response.

He snatched her to him and crushed her mouth with
punishing force. Shock rippled along her nerves. Before
she could react to the almost painful pressure of his lips
and his grip, his hold on her upper arms relaxed. The kiss
softened, becoming persuasive, and her traitorous body
welcomed his invading tongue, the hot exhalations on her
cheek, his thickening arousal against her abdomen. Her
heart raced, her skin moistened and heat collected in her
belly.

What was wrong with her? Why couldn't she push him
away and mean it? Why did the desire keep taking over?
This weekend she'd thought she'd been making him see
her point of view, but instead he'd been playing her like a
master violinist.

Xavier slowly eased back but only until his forehead
rested upon hers. His breaths still came rapidly. "Never
again refer to my child as a bastard."

"Our child."

"*Oui*. Our child." He lifted a hand and stroked her cheek,
then his thumb traced her lips as if in apology for the rough
handling. Every fiber of her being yearned to lean into his
touch, but she had to find the strength to push him away,
or else she'd become one of those women she pitied—the

mistresses who waited on the sidelines for their wealthy lovers to toss a crumb of attention their way.

"We are both tired, *mon amante*. Let us go to bed." His very male response pressed against her stomach said sleep would be a long time coming if she let him have his way. And she was tempted, so, *so* tempted. But then she'd have to deal with the aftermath of loathing herself for giving in.

Didn't he have a clue how much he was hurting her with his mixed signals? Probably not, because she'd done her best to hide her pain. She took two giant steps back. "No. At the risk of sounding like an old movie star, I want to be alone."

"We can be alone together, as we have done many times before to our mutual satisfaction."

"Maybe I'm being too polite since you're missing the point. I need a break. From you."

"A break? From me?"

"Yes, from you, Xavier."

"This is because of last night? But you enjoyed our little bondage game. Many times, I might add."

She gritted her teeth, hating the fact that he was right.

"Why did you cry last night?"

She fought to conceal her shock and embarrassment. "I didn't."

"The sheet was wet."

"That was sweat. You gave me quite a workout. That's why I want you to leave, Xavier. I need a break. I'm tired." *Of you. Of fighting my feelings. Of trying to act as if you're not tearing me to pieces.*

His brow pleated. "You are playing a dangerous game."

"I'm done playing. This weekend I tried to pretend there was nothing between us but sex because that's what you seem to believe. And I thought I could show you that you're wrong. But making love with you and trying to keep my heart out of it didn't teach *you* anything. I, however, learned a hard lesson. Being with you like that when you're still committed to her hurts too much. I can't do it anymore. I don't want to spend any more nights with you, and my horses and I will not be traveling to any more horse shows with you.

"What we have is so much more than sex, Xavier, and until you can see that, I can't sleep with you again. And while I appreciate your willingness to compromise and offer me a fraction of the year with my child, I can't live with that, either. Get out."

Hot. Cold. Push. Pull.

Xavier seethed as he climbed from the helicopter and walked the short distance across the Monaco tarmac to the waiting limo. He did not understand Megan's vacillatory behavior. As he had told her repeatedly, his engagement had not changed the rules of their relationship. She had.

He wanted things to return to the way they used to be, when she'd welcomed him with open arms and exuberance no matter what time of day or night he arrived, no matter his mood, his dress, his mental state or his intent. Like a good mistress should.

He missed her unguarded smiles, the conversations when she did not pause to consider each word before speaking. He missed being able to relax in her presence. He wanted to go back to the days when he could buy her gifts without her looking at him with suspicion.

She was one of those rare women who asked for nothing and took nothing for granted—the kind of woman a man enjoyed spoiling. Even if she had been right to question his motives because this time he had had an ulterior purpose for the designer apparel and horse show parties. He had to respect her cleverness in seeing through his weekend scheme. But then he had never doubted Megan's intelligence.

She was right about something else, too. What they had was definitely more than sex. But it was most emphatically *not* love.

Love was a desperate need to be with someone to the point of letting all else go—friendships, work, obligations, the roof over your head. Love was blind to faults. The fact that he could easily list each of Megan's proved he was not in love with her. Her stubbornness. Her extremely competitive nature. Her predilection for junk food. Her tendencies to overanalyze everything and lose track of time when she was with her horses.

He definitely did not love her. As she had rightly accused, he could not—*would* not—love anyone. He refused to become weak and subservient. He would do right by his child and make certain it never wanted for anything. Children did not need indulgent love. They needed discipline, food on the table and security. Love could be taken away too easily.

Megan claimed she loved him. But how could she, when even his mother could not?

Megan could not deny she desired him and enjoyed his company. All he had to do to get back into her good graces was to say three words. Lie. Something he had never done with Megan or anyone else. Honor—honesty—was everything to him.

Non, he would not lie to get Megan back in his bed. She would come to her senses soon enough and realize that they could share many good times in the coming months. Knowing their days were limited would only intensify the pleasure. She would likely come around as quickly as she had fallen into his arms after their initial separation. Possibly even by the time he returned home in a few days once he had attended to urgent business matters at the perfumery.

However, Megan had said something last night that caught his attention and prompted him to call the pilot for an impromptu trans-Atlantic flight. He had not informed Cecille of his impending fatherhood. As his future wife, she deserved to hear the news from him and not through gossip. She would not be getting only him as part of their marriage bargain. His *bébé* would be sharing the Alexandre Estate with them. And that was not the kind of information one shared via phone, email or text message.

Cecille had not been pleased by his demand that she fit him into her busy social schedule on short notice, but she had acquiesced. She had, however, insisted he meet her at a chic Monte Carlo café where their brunch would easily run him six hundred Euros. And she would insist on sitting on the patio—in the shade to protect her skin, of course—where she could see and be seen by all the right people. He had no problem with that. Image and connections were important.

At times like this, she acted very much like the demanding only child of a billionaire. Debussey had admitted he had spoiled her since at his advanced age he had given up on having an heir by the time his third wife became pregnant. There were rumors that Cecille might not be biologically his, a fact the perfumier vehemently denied. But no matter Cecille's parentage, she was Debussey's heiress and the key to regaining the Alexandre Estate.

She would make Xavier a good wife. Not only was she exceptionally beautiful, but she also spoke four languages fluently, had a college degree, was well-traveled and she had proven to be an excellent hostess for her father. All key ingredients for the wife of a successful CEO.

Another seed that Megan had planted sprouted. He knew

what he was getting out of the arrangement, but what was Cecille's motivation for marrying a man ten years her senior? One who did not like to party as she did. One who detested tennis. One who did not love her.

He spotted her even before the limo pulled to the curb by the harborside café, her table strategically chosen, her blond hair artfully draped over one bare shoulder. She had angled her chair so that her long, crossed legs would garner the attention she believed they deserved.

Her predictability brought a smile to his lips. Yes, she was a bit vain, but deservedly so. Her beauty caused a passerby to do a double-take and stumble on the sidewalk. She had that effect on most men, and yet Xavier had never felt more than the same appreciation for her looks as he would for an exquisite painting. She and he lacked the explosive chemistry he shared with Megan.

But chemistry did not make a marriage. And fires that hot burned out over time—a fact his mother had proven and every woman Xavier had enjoyed since his first sexual encounter had confirmed.

The chauffeur opened the door. Xavier stepped onto the sidewalk and checked his watch. "I will be ready to return to the helipad in one hour."

The driver bowed slightly. "*Oui,* Monsieur Alexandre."

Cecille spotted him and donned an attractive pout as he reached her side. He kissed her cheeks—not because he wanted to avoid her mouth, but to spare her lipstick, he assured himself with only a prick of conscience.

"*Bonjour,* Cecille."

"*Bonjour,* Xavier. What is so urgent that I had to postpone my appointment at the chocolatier?"

"You make appointments to buy chocolate?"

"I am ordering specially designed confections for each place setting at our wedding dinner."

This was one of those details, which Megan's cousin thought so important. He did not want to waste time on insignificant matters like a candy that would be forgotten the moment it was consumed or left behind because the guest watched her diet.

The waiter offered her a menu, but she waved him away. Xavier noted she only had sparkling water in front of her. "Do you not care to order?"

"Oh, no. I have to lose weight before the wedding."

She was already quite slim. Megan would have been poring over the menu looking for something new and unusual to try.

"Are you enjoying the wedding preparations?"

Cecille's perfect smile and carefully made-up eyes brightened. "Who doesn't enjoy planning an extravagant event for which one will be the star?"

Him, for one. But he could see how that would appeal to her. She gesticulated as she prattled on about her plans. Her diamond engagement ring caught and refracted the sunlight with each graceful sweep of her hands. He studied her slender fingers, her long, manicured nails, her pale, flawless skin.

So different from Megan's.

Megan's nails were short and usually clean, but never painted. She had a spattering of tiny almost unnoticeable scars across the backs and palms, gained from a lifetime of working with horses. Megan's hands were strong enough to control the powerful mounts she rode and yet gentle enough, seductive enough to drive him mad with desire. Megan did not shirk hard work, whereas he was certain Cecille would pay someone to sweat for her.

The women could not be more dissimilar. Megan would have no interest in the ring Cecille had chosen—a five-carat emerald-cut white diamond solitaire surrounded by yellow diamonds. If Megan ever married, her husband would be lucky to get her to wear a simple wedding band. She claimed jewelry got in her way and she rarely wore more than small stud earrings and a practical watch—a lesson he had learned early on in their association when he had tried to give her expensive pieces. She had refused to accept them, claiming the likelihood of her losing or damaging them was too high.

The sun crept around the edge of the building. Cecille shifted her chair to keep it in the shade. Megan never avoided the sun. She slathered on sunscreen—when she remembered—and relished the good weather which allowed her to ride without potentially hazardous mud beneath her horses' hooves. He suspected she cared more for the horses' safety than her own.

Cecille was graceful, articulate and elegant. Megan was an agile athlete who had been schooled by experience. She preferred to listen rather than talk, and she could read people better than any trained psychiatrist. Both women were confident, but Megan's assurance came from the belief that she could and had handled anything life threw at her. She was used to taking care of herself without a father or anyone else to bail her out of a tight spot. In fact, she had trouble accepting help because she disliked feeling indebted—a sentiment he understood all too well.

Cecille, on the other hand, had her father's wealth to smooth any of life's difficulties. If she found herself in trouble, she would call her father…and soon Xavier. Megan would attack the problem herself and—

"Xavier," Cecille interrupted his thoughts. "I asked if you agree."

He blinked and realized he had tuned out her chatter about the wedding preparations. *"Pardon?* Agree to what?"

Irritation flashed briefly across her face. She masked

it quickly with a radiant but saccharine smile. "I said I have chosen swans with interlocking necks to decorate the chocolates and the wedding cake. The same shape will be carved into an ice sculpture for the reception. Don't you agree the motif will be beautiful?"

Interlocking swans? "I am certain that every choice you make will be as lovely and elegant as you, Cecille. But as you have said, all eyes will be on the bride."

She flushed and beamed as he'd known she would. Megan would have given him hell for dodging the question. But he was not with Megan. He was with his fiancée. The woman he planned to marry in less than a year's time.

"Why did you agree to this marriage, Cecille? We are under no illusions that this is a love match."

Her lips parted in surprise. "Didn't Papa tell you? He promised to let me be the face for the new perfume if I married you."

No, Debussey had not shared that fact. But no matter, Cecille would be a good spokesperson and a beautiful advertisement for everything a woman wanted to be— young, gorgeous, rich enough to afford the product's high price tag. "You wish to be a model?"

"It is all I have ever wanted. I only went to college because Papa threatened to disown me if I didn't."

How had he not known this about the woman he intended to marry? But although they had been acquainted for five years, they had spent very little time alone together. Usually they attended dinner parties or her father was present, both circumstances that kept personal conversation to a minimum.

"There are more traditional means to achieving your career goal than marrying."

She glanced away. "I have tried to break into modeling

on my own. I have a portfolio and everything. But I have had little luck."

With her looks and her father's influence, there had to be a reason she had not succeeded. He doubted she had the work ethic required to become a model. He had dated several and knew each possessed a drive and stubborn determination that far exceeded anything Cecille had displayed to date. An attitude similar to Megan's.

"Is that why you needed to speak to me so urgently?" she prompted. "To ask why I'm marrying you?"

"Non." There was no way to finesse the news. He preferred to get to the point. "I asked to see you because I have recently learned that my mistress is pregnant. I preferred to inform you before you heard it elsewhere."

Her smile faltered but only briefly. "Is she going to get rid of it?"

"Non."

"Are you sure the baby is yours?"

"I am." It surprised him that she did not ask if he intended to keep his mistress after the wedding, but then many men in their social strata maintained both mistresses and families. "Since my decision to take custody of the child affects you, you have a right to know."

Heavily mascaraed—and possibly artificial—lashes descended once, twice, a third time. Her glossy painted lips pursed. "You want it?"

"Yes."

"Xavier, I'm not…really into children. You absolutely must promise me you'll hire someone to look after it. A nanny or a nurse or something until it's old enough for boarding school."

Boarding school. He had not thought that far ahead. As a child he had yearned for boarding school and begged to be shipped far away from the local village schoolboys who teased him unmercifully about his mother's rejection. But the idea of sending his child—Megan's child—away, though practical, did not appeal in the least.

"I will contract an agency to begin searching for a nanny, but I cannot promise that boarding school will be an option. I would like to know my son or daughter and raise the child with the knowledge of the Parfums Alexandre business."

Cecille fiddled with her silverware, something a woman with her poise rarely did. "I'm glad this came up, Xavier, because there's something you should know. I don't think I want to have children."

Another conversation they had yet to have. "Ever?"

"I really have no desire to bear a child. I think I'm missing that maternal whatever it is that some women have. And I'm certainly not the cookie-baking type. In fact, I don't cook at all. And the idea of snotty noses and dirty diapers holds no appeal. Maybe when I'm old, like thirty-five or something, then I might reconsider. If you insist. But men don't lose their figures when they become parents. And you don't have to concern yourself with the day-to-day drudgery of parenthood and whiny children. So I'd really rather not have any children unless we can adopt like the movie stars do and have a full-time child care staff."

He frowned as he considered her impassioned speech. She brought up several points. Megan would never complain about the messiness of motherhood and she enjoyed cooking. He could picture her now with a flour-covered child in the kitchen. He pushed the image away.

"I am thirty-five. Do I seem old to you?"

Her hesitation did not sit well. "Not really. I mean, you're still in decent shape. But you don't like to go out and have a good time. I can do that without you."

"My wife will not conduct herself at nightclubs like a single woman."

"I'm not staying home every night and playing hausfrau."

Non, Cecille certainly did not possess the maternal urge that made Megan fight like a lioness to keep her child. Which meant Megan's child would be his only heir.

He must get custody. Failure was not an option.

And he and his future bride still had much to work out about their pending marriage.

Megan jerked awake and lay in the bed, trying to figure out what had roused her. No sounds disturbed the silent, dark cottage, and she had remembered to lock her doors. She checked the bedside clock. Four.

Then she felt a funny flutter in her tummy. What the—?

The baby.

A burst of adrenaline instantly eradicated her sleepiness. She pressed her palm to the spot below her navel, held her breath and waited for it to happen again. And then it did. A sensation like the soft sweep of butterfly wings or the flip of a goldfish's tail stirred deep inside her, making her practically giddy with excitement.

When it ceased, she rolled toward the cell phone on the bedside table and stopped. Hannah would be sleeping. Who else could she call? She had to tell someone. She hadn't announced her pregnancy yet, so there was no one else.

Except Xavier.

Her pulse raced faster. The baby wiggled more. This was too big of a deal not to share. She grabbed her phone and speed-dialed his number.

"Allô." The sound of his voice made her heart skip, but then the fact that he'd used the generic *allô* instead of greeting her by one of the pet names he usually used

registered. Her name would have come up on his caller ID. He never greeted her with *allô*.

"Xavier— The baby— You won't believe what just happened." Exhilaration mingled with her confusion over the greeting, muddling her thoughts and words. She didn't know how to describe the sensation or her excitement.

"The *bébé?* Megan, what happened?"

"Megan? Is that her? Your mistress?" A husky female voice asked in French in the background.

Megan's euphoria vaporized. "Are you with *her?* Your fiancée?"

A moment of silence stretched between them. *"Oui."*

Jealousy rose like bile in her throat. Hearing his fiancée's voice slammed home the reality that Megan might not win this competition. Up until now, at least a part of her had believed she had a chance at victory.

"Never mind. It's nothing. I'm sorry I bothered you." Megan disconnected the call and curled up in a ball, hugging a pillow to her middle.

Xavier was with *her*. The woman good enough to be his wife. And the last thing he'd want to hear about was the baby he'd never intended to make with Megan. The baby he would have asked her to get rid of if he'd known sooner.

Eight

With apprehension crushing his stomach like a brawler's fist, Xavier pounded on Megan's front door. The darkened cottage and empty driveway were not good signs when combined with the odd tone of her voice when she had called and his inability to reach her by phone afterward.

The foyer light clicked on and the door opened. Megan stood in the narrow gap. He scanned her from head to toe, searching for whatever could be amiss. "Are you and the *bébé* all right?"

Looking mussed and sleepy but otherwise perfectly healthy in her running shorts, T-shirt and bare feet, she swept back her tousled hair. "Of course. Why wouldn't we be?"

Fear retreated, forced out by anger. "You did not answer your phone any of the dozen times I tried to call you back."

Her expression turned defiant. "I told you it wasn't important."

"You sounded upset."

"I wasn't upset. I was excited."

"Why?"

"Xavier, it's late. I'm not up to butting heads with you tonight. Can't this wait until tomorrow?"

"I left my fiancée sitting alone in a Monaco café, and I canceled a series of urgent business meetings with my executive staff to jet across the Atlantic to ensure you and the *bébé* were safe."

As soon as he heard the words coming from his mouth, the reality of what he had done dropped on him like a massive boulder. He had abandoned his work and his future wife for Megan.

But the panic that had gripped him throughout the flight because she had not answered her phone did not mean he loved her. His concern was solely for his child, the future heir of Parfums Alexandre.

"Nobody asked you to race back."

His fingers fisted, released, fisted, released in frustration over her stonewalling. "I am not leaving until you tell me why you called and hung up on me."

She scowled at him. There were smudges beneath her eyes and a droop to her shoulders that he rarely saw. "Are you certain you are well? You looked tired."

She slapped a hand to her chest and fluttered her lashes—unmascaraed lashes—dramatically. "Your flattery makes my heart pitter-patter. If I look tired it's because I've been up since four."

He calculated the time difference. "You called me at four."

"I didn't know who else to call, but don't worry, I won't make the mistake of disturbing you and your fiancée again." She tried to close the door. He stopped her by sticking his shoe in the gap.

Her continued avoidance of the issue threatened to snap his composure. "Megan—"

She held up a hand and sighed. "Oh, for pity's sake. Come in. But don't get comfortable. You're not staying."

He ignored her inhospitable words and followed her into the cottage. She picked up a small quilt from the sofa and folded it, then straightened the throw pillows and a stack of magazines. Baby and pregnancy magazines.

She bent to gather a jar of peanut butter and a banana peel, but he caught her shoulders to stop her bustling about. The urge to pull her close came over him. He attributed it to relief that she was okay, but that did not explain why, when he had barely been gone twenty-four hours, returning filled him with a sense of coming home. Home. To this place. Her temporary residence.

In the past, Megan would have greeted him by twining her arms around his neck, pressing her body against his and kissing him until they were both breathless. But not tonight. Tonight she looked as if she could not wait for him to leave—a circumstance that lit a fire under his already simmering temper.

"Why did you call, Megan?"

Her expression turned mulish. He expected her to refuse to answer, then she bit her lip and tried to shrug off his hold, but he held fast. "I felt the baby move for the first time."

His heart skipped a beat. His gaze dropped to her stomach. His hand followed. She tried to back away but he held her captive with his right hand, covering her belly with his left. Her body heat seeped into his palm and then invaded the rest of him.

She pushed at his arm. "You won't be able to feel it externally for weeks yet. I can barely feel it."

"What does it feel like?"

"It's a fluttery thing deep inside. Like a fish breaking

the water of a pond with his tail. The articles say babies are most noticeably active at night when the mother lies still. That's why I was lying down on the sofa when you arrived. I was waiting for the baby to move again. I guess I fell asleep."

Her excitement sparked an inexplicable yearning to share her experiences and to see her body ripen with child. His child. Odd because he had never harbored such thoughts before about anyone. But he wanted to see his son or daughter grow, feel it kicking with impatience to get out and make its mark on the world.

"I do not care what the magazines say. I want to try to feel it move."

"Xavier—"

"Ten minutes. Lie with me for ten minutes then I will leave you to your beauty sleep. Not that you need it. You are always lovely. Especially now. Pregnancy has made your skin luminescent."

She exhaled an exasperated breath. "Don't even try—"

He held up a hand. "Please. I wish to feel our baby move or to at least share the experience with you."

How different she was from Cecille who would have preened at his compliments.

Her shoulders slumped. "All right. C'mon. But no funny business."

He followed her to the bedroom, ignoring his quickening pulse. He was not here for sex. Although he would not turn it down if she offered. And he was certain he could persuade her out of her clothes if he were so inclined. But he had been almost forty hours without sleep. They would both enjoy the intimacy more after he had rested.

She lay on top of the burgundy-and-gold spread. He kicked off his shoes and stretched out beside her in the dark room. She turned on the bedside lamp, but the Tiffany stained-glass light did little to chase away the shadows.

He rolled onto his side and placed a hand on her stomach. She curled her fingers around his and shifted his hand lower—to the place where the elastic band of her panties usually rested. That band was noticeably absent tonight and the fact that she was naked beneath her thin shorts spiked his temperature and pulse rate.

Rather than pull away, she left her palm resting on the back of his hand. Her scent enveloped him, stirring his awareness and making him rethink his decision to delay gratification until after he had rested. But any sexual overtures would get him escorted to the door.

"Is he moving?"

"Not yet. That's what woke me this morning. His or her wiggling. It was just so *amazing.* I wasn't expecting it, and it was too early to call Hannah. But I had to tell someone and I didn't know who else to call so I called you. I'm sorry." Her words gushed out like water through a broken pipe.

"I am glad you called me."

She turned her head on the pillow to look at him. "Even though I interrupted your date with your future wife?"

"Oui." The hurt she tried and failed to hide pricked something inside him. It should not. He reminded himself— not for the first time—that he had made no promises and broken none. But his discomfort was undeniable.

"I flew to Monaco to tell Cecille about *le bébé.*" Megan would not be happy to hear her worries confirmed.

"What did she say?"

He could not lie. "She informed me she does not wish to have children. Your baby—our *bébé*—will be my only child."

She shifted again, staring up at the ceiling. "Mine, too. As you said, children and the circuit are not a good mix.

By the time I'm too old to compete I'll be too old to have more children."

He should not feel relieved. But he did, even though that meant denying Megan another chance at motherhood. "Tell me when he moves."

"I will. But everything I've read says it's too soon for you to feel anything."

"Tell me anyway." He would live vicariously through her excitement.

They lay silently side by side not touching except for his hand on her belly, and Xavier realized he missed holding her—even the nights when sex was not on the agenda, few though they might be. He listened to the sound of her breathing as it slowed and knew the exact moment she drifted off to sleep. It was only then that he realized he had done this—listened to her succumb to slumber—often enough to recognize her breathing patterns. He could not remember ever having done so with any other lover.

Her hand became heavy on his and her face relaxed. His gaze shifted to her bedside clock. His ten minutes were up. But if he left he would wake her. She needed her rest. He would close his eyes for a few moments and enjoy her company. Once she entered a deeper level of sleep, he would be able to leave. A smile curved his lips. When she reached that level of sleep he could move the house without waking her.

But for now he was right where he wanted to be. And in the coming months he would remain as close as Megan would allow him to be until the last possible moment— when he must return home for his wedding.

With his son or daughter.

Megan halfheartedly flipped through a pregnancy magazine as the sun pinked the sky outside her window and tried not to think about the man sleeping in her bed. Or the roller coaster of emotions he'd put her through. Again.

When Xavier had knocked on her door last night, she'd hated him. The animosity had burned her stomach like bad chili.

She'd hated him because he'd left her to fly off to be with his fiancée.

She'd hated him because he was putting his business and his greed ahead of their baby.

She'd hated him for breaking her and making her beg for his possession after the horse show.

Mostly she'd hated him for not loving her.

But when she'd opened the door, the concern etching lines in his face had cracked the wall around her heart just a little. His confession that he'd left his bride-to-be and jetted back to Megan's side because he was worried about her had widened the gap, flooding her with hope and joy.

And then the awe and anticipation on his face as he'd lay motionless beside her last night, his respirations shallow and his body tensed with anticipation, had chiseled away yet another piece of her protective barricade.

When he'd held her, simply held her with no sexual overtures, her will to resist him had crumbled and she'd had her first good night's sleep since learning of his engagement, wrapped in the strong arms of the man she loved.

But just because she was rested didn't mean she was going to be a pushover. Her baby's well-being came first.

A pair of hummingbirds outside the window pulled her attention away from the magazine she hadn't been able to concentrate on. She'd read the same paragraph about preventing leg cramps three times and didn't remember a word of it.

The birds, each trying to outsmart and outmaneuver the

other, darted and dashed in pursuit of the single daylily bloom and the nectar it harbored. Their battle seemed symbolic of her fight with Xavier over their baby.

But both birds could get sustenance if they learned to share. And as much as she hated to admit it, that was probably the only way to solve her problem, too.

Xavier's concern and his excitement over the baby's movement had proven he would be an interested parent, and her baby deserved two of those because, God forbid, sometimes tragedy struck. She and Hannah were proof of that. Two parents were insurance and therefore definitely better than one. The chance of losing both parents at once, as she had, was rare.

Hannah had had her father to fall back on after her mother's death in a riding accident. But Megan had only had an uncle who had resented her existence. If not for Hannah and Nellie, the housekeeper who'd taken a motherly role, Megan's life would have been very bleak and devoid of love.

For her baby's sake, she couldn't exclude Xavier from her—*their*—child's life.

Not even if he married *her*—the beautiful, rich, educated fiancée who was everything Megan was not.

But his admission that his future wife didn't want children had intensified Megan's fear that her child might be raised in a cold, loveless environment. She'd only suffered five years of that. She couldn't imagine a lifetime of being unwanted and in the way. But if Cecille didn't want children of her own, she certainly wouldn't want a mistress's child underfoot.

A true no-win situation.

To keep Xavier in her baby's life, Megan would have to compromise. And she detested compromising. In her mind, compromise equated to quitting. Settling for less than the best. Less than winning.

She desperately needed an acceptable alternative that would prevent her child from being raised in a hostile environment—and one that would avoid the risk of a foreign parent's refusal to honor a shared custody agreement.

And despite racking her brain for the past half hour, she'd only come up with one solution—one that didn't satisfy her at all because it meant living in the shadow of Xavier's perfect wife and enduring the gossip that would follow her and her baby around the Grand Prix circuit. But until she found a better alternative, it would have to do. And sooner or later the gossip would die down. Wouldn't it?

A sound jerked her gaze toward the bedroom. Xavier strolled barefoot into the den, looking totally unlike his usual suave self. She had never seen him in rumpled clothing before, and unfortunately his beard-stubbled face, mussed hair and heavy-lidded eyes were both endearing and sexy as sin.

"Good morning," he offered in a raspy morning voice that tweaked her heartstrings and made her yearn for those magical days before she'd learned of his engagement, before he'd destroyed her fairy-tale life. "I fell asleep."

"You slept hard. You missed me getting up to go to the bathroom at two and getting up for good at six."

"You could have woken me."

That would have meant facing him when she felt vulnerable. No way. "You obviously needed the rest."

"I apologize. I told you I would leave last night."

His unexpected apology took her aback. Xavier didn't apologize. But then, never making a wrong move—other than this stupid engagement—didn't require apologies or excuses.

She tossed aside her magazine and rose, determined to level the playing field. She would face him eye-to-eye or at least as close as their six-inch height difference would allow.

"I've decided I want you to be a part of our child's life. I'm going to move back to France. But not until after the baby is born. Until then, I have obligations here to Hannah and to my students. But I won't live in the cottage where I'll have to watch your wife come and go."

"You will not need to move. We shall be living elsewhere."

Her heart dropped. He was moving? "Where?"

"To the Alexandre estate."

"You have another property?"

"It is one my father sold when he fell into financial difficulties."

"And you're buying it back?"

"Something like that."

Unable to comprehend that he hadn't told her he was moving and the shocking, irrational sense of loss that accompanied that knowledge, Megan shook her head. But then again, he hadn't told her he was marrying another woman, either.

"Wherever you live, I won't stay in the house you and I decorated together. I'll find another place, another stable and another sponsor. But I'm coming back only on one condition."

He stiffened. "And that condition is…?"

"I want sole custody. You can have unlimited visitation rights, but the visits will take place in my home. I will not allow our child to stay at your estate."

His expression darkened. "That is unreasonable."

"Your fiancée doesn't want children of her own. She's not going to want your mistress's child around."

"I will hire a nanny."

"*We* will hire a nanny, and I get the final vote on who gets the job. But a nanny is not a mother. I spent years of my life trying to gain my uncle's approval. When that didn't work, I fought to gain his respect by becoming more like him than his own daughter. But no matter what I did, it was never enough. He resented my presence. I always knew he didn't want me. The situation became intolerable, and I left the States for Europe as soon as I legally could. I refuse to allow my child to grow up believing he or she is somehow flawed and unlovable."

She winced when she realized how revealing the last statement had been. She hadn't meant to let that slip.

"You are not unlovable, Megan."

"Are you saying you love me?"

His eyes filled with regret, giving her the answer even before he opened his mouth. "If I could love anyone, it would be you."

The words cut deep. "Then you admit you won't be able to love our child."

He mashed his lips together so hard they almost disappeared. "The child will lack for nothing."

"Materially."

"What you propose is not acceptable."

"It's the only compromise I'm willing to make."

"Any judge will grant me joint custody at the least."

"Any French judge, maybe. But this baby will be an American citizen, born on American soil. No American judge will grant you joint custody when he hears your marriage is a business arrangement and that you'll be taking my child out of the country."

"My child will be a French citizen, as well."

"I won't give up guardianship without a fight."

He shoved his hand through his hair and turned toward the window. "I have to marry Cecille."

"Why? Is she pregnant, too?" The idea of that hurt too much to bear.

He scowled at her. "I have told you. I have not slept with her or anyone else since meeting you."

"Then why? I don't see anyone holding a gun to your head. Are you in financial trouble?"

"Of course not. I—" A muscle in his jaw ticked. "I vowed to my father that I would right his mistakes. And I have all except for one—regaining the Alexandre Estate."

He wasn't making sense. "How is the estate connected to Cecille?"

"Her father owns it."

"So buy it back."

"Monsieur Debussey refuses to sell. The only way I can regain the property is by marrying his daughter. Then he will deed the property to me."

"That's crazy."

"Possibly. But he is an old man with health problems, and he wants to ensure that his only child and his business are in good hands before he dies."

"You're taking over Debussey's perfume empire, too?"

"Yes. I will be CEO of Parfums Alexandre et Debussey."

His avarice astounded her. "So you're marrying a woman you don't love and trading your happiness, your future and your baby's future for a piece of land and what amounts to a promotion. What about Cecille? Doesn't she deserve the right to find the right man and fall in love?"

"You keep harping about love. Love does not last, Megan. Honor and security do."

How sad was that? Xavier not only didn't love her, but he didn't believe in love at all. "How is it honorable to marry for material gain?"

"The plans have been set in motion, the announcements made. I will not humiliate Cecille by rejecting her the way that my father did his fiancée."

"Your father broke an engagement? Thirty-something years ago, I'm guessing. And you are still trying to fix that?"

"He blackened our family name and cost us the estate."

"This is beginning to sound like a bad soap opera. How is his past related to your…catastrophe-in-the-making?"

"Parfums Alexandre was having financial difficulties before my birth. My father made an alliance with an investor. He would marry the daughter in return for a loan to float the company."

"Wait a minute. You're telling me your father married for money, too?"

"He should have. But he left his bride at the altar and ran away with my mother—the family maid—whom he claimed he loved and whom he had gotten pregnant. A week later, his jilted bride drove her car head-on into a tree. Many claim she could not live with the shame."

"That is tragic. But your father chose love over money. And he chose to parent you. That's to be admired not reviled."

"My parents' so-called love was short-lived. When the company continued to struggle, my father was forced to sell the estate. My mother fell out of love when she had to move to a modest apartment and curb her spending. She fled with my father's wealthy best friend."

Bewildered, Megan shook her head. How had she never known this? "How old were you?"

"Two. But that is irrelevant. I must restore honor to the Alexandre name."

"That sounds positively medieval. You're not responsible

for your parents' choices, Xavier. Just as your father is not responsible for his former fiancée's."

"She died because of him."

"She died because she made a bad decision."

"You do not understand what it is like to live under the shadow of such a scandal."

"No. Maybe I don't. But I do recognize honor when I see it. Your father chose not to turn his marriage into hypocrisy. You, on the other hand, plan to stand in the front of a church and promise God and your witnesses to love, honor and cherish Cecille. I don't think you know the meaning of those words."

He flinched. "French law does not require a religious ceremony."

"So you won't be lying to a higher power. But you'll still be lying. There's no honor in that. Don't do this. Please. For your child's sake, for my sake, don't marry Cecille."

"I will not renege on my promise."

"Even if I told you I loved you?"

His silence gave her the answer.

She walked to the front door and opened it. "Then get your shoes and get out. And forget about my offer to move back to France. I thought you could be a positive part of our child's life. But I was wrong. My God, Xavier, you're no more than a corporate prostitute. I don't want my child to learn those kinds of values. I'm suing you for sole custody."

Nine

Heart sinking, Megan stared at the attorney Wyatt had recommended and hoped—*prayed*—she'd misheard. "How can a simple custody case cost seven figures?"

"It is never simple to deny a parent access to his child, and since said child is Mr. Alexandre's only heir and his arranged marriage, though not admirable, is not illegal you can expect him to pursue this until he finds a sympathetic judge. If you win, he'll appeal. Repeatedly. If he wins, you will. Custody battles tend to get even uglier than divorces. A child brings out the best and the worst in people. You definitely won't get out of this for less than six figures, but I'm guessing it'll be more, and expect the wrangling to go on for years. It will consume your life. His legal team is top-notch."

"I was told *you* were the best."

Mr. Stein's smile resembled a shark's. Toothy. Predatory. "I am. I always get the best deal for my clients. That's why

I'm recommending you accept Mr. Alexandre's offer of joint custody."

A prickle of unease crept up her spine like a spider and the sting of betrayal slipped beneath her ribs like a stiletto. "You're advising me to settle?"

"There's a lot of money in it for you if you do. A monthly allowance. Child support. He's agreed to pay the nanny's salary, the child's educational expenses and so on, as we've already covered. You wanted the best deal, Ms. Sutherland. This is it." He tapped the thick pile of papers on his desk. "He's being very generous."

"But I'd only get a few months of the year. The best deal for me is sole custody of my child. I want to fight this."

"You're unlikely to win."

"I thought you'd never lost a case."

"I haven't."

Settling meant compromising, and in this case that wasn't going to work. "What you're telling me is that you always sell out before you can lose."

His face hardened and his toothpaste-ad smile faded. "As I've said, Ms. Sutherland, I always get the best deal for my clients. Sometimes that means *settling* out of court before their pride makes them spend a lot of money and come out with even less than the initial offering."

The condescending jerk. Megan drew a sharp breath to tell him pride had nothing to do with it, but before she could the phone beside him chirped.

He pushed a button. "Yes, Elizabeth?"

"Mr. Alexandre and his team are here."

He checked his watch. "Right on time. Send them in."

The attorney looked at Megan. "I need your permission to accept this deal now."

Heart racing, she weighed her options. Nothing had changed. She couldn't allow her child to be raised in the

environment Xavier and his bought bride would provide.
"You're not going to get it. I want sole custody."

"Can you afford that, Ms. Sutherland?" he asked in
a patronizing tone that made her want to wipe the floor
with him. Her competitors, the ones who knew her well,
wouldn't dare speak to her that way.

Challenging Xavier could very well cost her everything,
but to keep her son or daughter from feeling unloved or
unwanted, it would be worth it. "Yes. And don't under-
estimate me or try to sell me out again, Mr. Stein, or I'll
find another attorney. Is that clear?"

His eyebrows shot up in a quick show of surprise, then
his expression turned to one of grudging respect. "Yes,
Ms. Sutherland."

The door opened. Xavier looked like a winner from the
moment he strode in with his customary I-own-the-world
swagger and his designer suit.

Her heart skipped. Even with all they'd been through,
she'd missed him these past two weeks. And sadly, she still
loved him, if the tightness in her chest was any indication.

Masochist.

Why had he sacrificed their fairy-tale romance on the
money altar?

His green gaze met hers. Hard and inflexible. She gave
him her best game-on challenging glare. She thought she
caught a twinge of regret in his eyes, but he turned to pull
out a chair at the opposite end of the board table before she
could be sure. A team of three equally formidable suit-clad
men took the remaining seats.

Once all the men were seated, Mr. Stein folded his hands
atop the file folder. "Gentlemen, Mr. Alexandre, thank you
for coming here today. But I regret to inform you that Ms.
Sutherland has decided to decline your offer."

Stunned silence filled the room, then Xavier's gaze met hers. "I would like to speak to Megan alone."

"Sir, I don't advise—" one of Xavier's team began, but Xavier sliced him a look that staunched the words.

Her attorney hiked a questioning eyebrow. Megan nodded. He rose. "Gentlemen, this way please."

As soon as the door closed behind them, Xavier bolted to his feet and stalked to the wall of windows overlooking the street fifty stories below. Hands on his hips, he pivoted. "You can't afford this fight."

She remained seated behind the protective barrier of the conference table. Even though that gave him the height advantage, she couldn't risk his touch undermining her decision. "I can't afford *not* to fight. I want what's best for my son or daughter and I will get it even if I have to sell everything I own, including my horses. Each one of them is worth a couple of million."

Shock and disbelief flickered in his eyes. "Riding is your life."

"I'll still have the opportunity to ride someone else's horses."

He frowned. "Commander's Belle is the last foal born of your father's stallion. You've raised her from birth. She is your livelihood and your ticket to the world equestrian trials."

He remembered. And for some stupid reason that made her eyes sting. Stupid pregnancy hormones. "Yes, she's a direct descendent of my father's horse, and I am definitely attached to her. But this baby is a direct descendant of my father—one I will fight you till my last breath to keep."

"Even though doing so could bankrupt you."

"You just don't get it, do you, Xavier? Money is not the most important thing. Having a family and someone to love is."

"Love does not last."

"I hope you're right. Because I want to stop loving you."

He flinched as if she'd slapped him, then searched her face. "I do not understand you, Megan Sutherland."

Then he turned and stalked out the door through which the men had exited. Another piece of her heart crumbled. But she couldn't afford to be weak now. She'd just taken on the fight of her life.

Midnight.

Xavier sat back at his desk, rubbed his tired eyes and listened to the silence of Parfums Alexandre's facility while he rolled his stiff shoulders. The employees had long since gone home, but he had stayed to catch up on paperwork.

Even though he had been back a month, it had taken him this long to get back into a routine. He had plenty of projects needing his attention as a result of his sojourn to the States including the Alexandre/Debussey merger documents and the wedding guest list to review.

And no reason to go home.

Megan was right. They had shared more than sex. He had not realized how deeply she had infiltrated his existence until he had returned without her. Nor had he been aware of how eager he had been to leave the office each evening to be with her when she had lived here in her cottage.

But every time he returned home, he tripped over traces of her. A hair clip. One of the many books she had already read but could not seem to throw out. A bottle of her rose-scented lotion. A sock. This morning he'd found a pair of her lacy white panties in his suit pocket and the memory of how they had come to be there had lambasted him.

And then there were the turtles—figurines of all shapes, sizes, colors and materials that she had collected during their travels. Some were quite ugly. He would swear she bought every turtle they had passed and some of the trinkets had ended up in his home.

He had once asked her why the reptile fascinated her so. With hindsight he now realized she had avoided the question by slipping off her panties in the five-star restaurant—discreetly of course—and stuffing them into his pocket. He had been suitably distracted. Hence the lingerie he had found this morning.

What detail could be so personal that she would risk public humiliation to avoid revealing it?

And why was it only now that he realized she had done so? How many other times had she refused to share? How many other times had he failed to notice something obviously important to her? What else could he have missed? And why did he resent her secrets?

Why did it matter?

He pushed away from his desk and strolled toward the window, dark now except for the streetlights below. He had tried to resume his old life since returning. It lacked... something. He had taken Cecille to dinner three times and even endured attending a tennis match with her. Baking in the hot sun while men beat a yellow ball back and forth had not been an enjoyable experience.

He had not even minded when one of the players flirted shamelessly with her after the match. Had some buffoon made such overtures to Megan in his presence he would have—and had—ended such behavior immediately. Nor had he cared that Cecille flirted back.

So that would be his life. He and Cecille would exist separately. He would tolerate the occasional tennis match. She would suffer through a few of his horse shows. And in the evenings he would work and she would do...whatever it was she did. But he would have the Alexandre estate and soon, his son or daughter.

Oh, yes, he and Megan had shared much more than sex.

Megan would be five months pregnant now. Her baby belly more noticeable. And he wanted to see her—her belly—more than he wanted his next breath. He wanted to lay his hand on her warm flesh and feel his child move.

But only because it was his heir.

Restless but not tired enough to go home to bed, Xavier wandered to the sitting area, poured himself a scotch, then left it sitting on the bar untouched. Liquor was not the flavor for which he hankered.

He picked up a horse digest that had come last week—one he had not perused because he and Megan used to read it together. It was her favorite rag.

He sat on the leather sofa—the one he and Megan had had sex on numerous times—and absently flipped through the pages.

Megan. She haunted his thoughts. But only because they had unfinished business between them and he hated loose ends.

She would come to her senses and end this waiting game soon. What else could she possibly want? His offer had been more than generous—so generous in fact that his legal team had complained and cajoled, trying to get him to change the terms. He had not.

But Megan was a supreme strategist. No doubt she was plotting some way to get additional concessions from him. When she realized he would not give in, she would accept his terms. Her threat to sell her horses was an empty one. She loved those animals. They had been her family—the one she now claimed she required to be happy.

A picture of a familiar chestnut mare caught his eye. His hands stilled as he skimmed the glossy page.

Commander's Belle, For Sale.

His chest tightened. Megan had not been bluffing.

He scrambled in his pocket for his cell phone and dialed her number. "Hello."

Her voice, hard to distinguish over the loud music in the background, took what remained of his breath. Where was she that she would be listening to music in the middle of the afternoon?

"You are selling Belle," he stated baldly.

"I told you I would."

"What of Rocky Start?"

"Already sold."

The band on his rib cage tightened. "To whom?"

"Xavier, I'm in the middle of something here. Was there a reason for your call?"

In the middle of what? A date? The idea burned his stomach and her cool, dismissive tone irritated him. He swallowed to ease the strange obstruction in his throat. "What is Belle's price?"

"Why do you need to know?"

"It is not listed in the advertisement."

"I repeat, why do you need to know?"

"Because I will take her—whatever your asking price."

The line went dead. He stared at the phone. Had they been disconnected or had Megan hung up on him? He suspected the latter. But he would not stoop to calling her back to ask. If they had been disconnected, she could contact him.

The phone remained silent.

He dropped it on the table and only then realized his heart was racing. Megan was selling all that was dear to her for his child. As she had told him she would.

She was not going to walk away from this baby. No matter the personal cost.

He snatched up the phone and dialed his stable manager. The man's groggy voice answered. "Megan has sold Rocky Start. Find out who bought him."

"Sir? It's…the middle of the night."

Xavier grimaced, frustrated he could not have his answers now. "Have the name on my desk first thing in the morning. Buy Rocky and also Commander's Belle. No matter the price."

"Yes, sir."

Xavier ended the call, shaking his head at the irony. By purchasing the mare he would be providing Megan the financial means to fight him for custody. But those horses were her family. She had raised both from weanlings. Trained them, pampered them, talked and hummed to them as she groomed and rode them.

He would return them to her with the codicil that she could not sell them again.

Because for the first time he understood what she had meant when she said it was not about the money.

Megan smiled at Hannah and shoved her phone back into her pocket.

Hannah leaned closer to be heard above the band auditioning for her wedding reception. "That's your turtle smile. What's going on?"

"Nothing."

Hannah gave her the you're-not-fooling-me look then signaled the band to stop playing. "Thank you. I'll get back to you after I've spoken to my fiancé."

She turned to Megan. "Let's go. You're not pulling into your shell and keeping secrets from me."

Hannah snapped up her belongings and strode briskly from the building. Megan tried to think of a way to keep from ruining what until now had been a fun day of them sampling cakes, looking at flowers and listening to potential entertainment. She came up with nothing.

The heat hit them like a wall as soon as they stepped outside. Megan stalled by studying the dark clouds gathering on the horizon. "Would you look at that? We're in for a bad storm."

"What did Xavier want?" Hannah asked as soon as the car doors closed, sealing them in privacy.

Megan sighed. She should tough this out on her own. Hannah had enough on her mind with the wedding. But she didn't have the strength. "He just offered to buy Belle."

"The bastard. Does he want to take everything from you?"

"Apparently. But don't sweat it. I hung up on him. And I'm not selling Belle to him no matter how much he offers."

Hannah made no attempt to put the car in motion. "That's the first time you've heard from him since the lawyer meeting a month ago?"

"Yes." Four weeks of silence. No counteroffers, no withdrawal of the deal as her lawyer had predicted.

"Do you hate him yet?"

"I hate this side of him and what he's doing." But she still missed him.

What if she sold both her horses, spent all her money and still lost the custody battle?

Don't think that way. Quitters never win.

"But you still love him?"

She nodded. "I love what we had. And I want that back. Doesn't that make me a first-class fool?"

Hannah reached across the car and grabbed Megan's hand. "No, Megs, it makes you a fool for love. Happens to the best of us. It certainly happened to me."

"The difference is you found your happy ending. I don't see that happening here."

Hannah moved her hand to Megan's baby bump. "Here's your happy ending. You're going to be a mom. The best damned mom on the planet. And we're not going to let him take that away from you. No matter what. And I am going to be the most amazing aunt ever."

Megan's lips smiled, but her heart was still breaking. Would she ever get over that man?

Xavier entered the barn beside his stable manager.

"He's not the horse we knew, sir. He's missing a little pep in his step."

"Missing a little pep in his step" described Xavier's condition exactly. He had been lethargic since his return from the States, but that was to be expected, given his late hours and heavier than usual workload and the pressure of the merger. And the marriage.

He stopped outside the stall holding Rocky Start—the same stall the horse had occupied before Megan had left France. The gelding whinnied in recognition.

Xavier opened the door and stepped inside. He stroked the horse's glossy neck. "Do you miss her, boy?"

I do, he finally allowed himself to admit.

And he wanted her back. Not just because of the *bébé.* He missed her company. He missed the way she teased and taunted him in a way that no one else would dare. He missed the look in her eyes that said she believed he could conquer the world, and he missed holding her as she fell asleep. He missed quiet mornings when they cooked breakfast and ate together in her cottage. He missed watching her compete and the pride he had felt that she was his woman.

He missed the way she loved him.

The admission made him feel weak. Like less of a man.

He turned to his employee. "What do you mean she refused to sell Belle?"

"She refused to sell the mare to *you*, sir."

"Did you meet her asking price?"

"I offered her more. She still refused."

"I want that mare."

"Do you mind if I ask why? Belle's a great horse, but she has some age on her and she's nearing the end of her career. And her price is high for a broodmare."

Why did he want Megan's horses? A good question.

He wasn't going to ride them. And having anyone but Megan show Belle seemed like sacrilege. Megan and Belle had been a team since Belle's first saddle. The two of them in motion were like a fine ballet. But his burning desire to possess both of her horses was undeniable.

If her horses were here, she would come to his stable to see them. And then he would give them to her, contingent on her boarding them here. In his barn.

He wanted Megan's horses because he wanted her back. The realization shook him. Head reeling, he offered the gelding a treat from his pocket—one of the treats Megan had left behind in his tack room. He needed time to think. Time to figure out why it was so bloody important to have Megan on his turf.

"Sir?"

"Just get that mare. Buy her anonymously through an agent if you must. But get her."

He stalked out of the barn. But his chaotic thoughts stampeded after him. He headed straight for the practice ring, vaguely noting the sun setting behind the oak trees. Dusk. Megan's favorite time of the day to ride. But the ring was empty. No equestrians cantered in and out of the shadows.

No Megan.

He wanted her back more than he wanted the Alexandre estate.

He wanted her back more than he wanted to be CEO of the largest privately owned perfumery in the world.

He wanted her back more than he wanted to prove that he was a better man, a smarter man than his father, one who would not jeopardize the roof over his head for infatuation.

He wanted Megan back because her leaving had left a vacant space in his heart that nothing had been able to fill.

He braced his arms against the rail and let the heavy weight of his thoughts settle over him. He wanted Megan back... Because he loved her.

Love.

Him.

Impossible.

Apparently not.

But to have Megan in his life, he would have to forfeit everything he had strived for over the past fifteen years. He would have to turn his back on his vow to regain the Alexandre estate, and he would have to repeat his father's mistake of jilting his bride-to-be.

As Megan had said, marrying Cecille for the material goods and status she could bring him was not the honorable thing to do. Releasing her from the bargain he had made with her father was.

Megan had the courage to sacrifice her horses and her career—everything she held dear—for their child. That was truly honorable. How could she respect him if he did not match her courage?

He hoped he was not too late to make amends.

But he had made promises. To Cecille. To her father. Promises he must break. He must speak to his lawyers and to Cecille and Monsieur Debussey. And then—and only then—could he go to Megan a free man.

Her man.

If she would have him.

Xavier stood in the grand foyer of the Alexandre mansion beside Monsieur Debussey and said goodbye to his dream of regaining ownership of the beautiful château.

But no matter how beautiful the house, it would never be a home without Megan and their child.

"Then we're agreed on terms?" he asked Debussey.

"*Oui.* I will sell you Parfums Debussey and in return, you will give Cecille the job as spokesperson for the new Debussey perfume."

"I will hire the best modeling coach available to coach her in her new job, but I won't tolerate unprofessional behavior or carry dead weight. If Cecille fails to deliver, I will have to let her go."

The older man inclined his head. "I understand. As you have said, I must teach her to survive after I am gone. Perhaps the best way to do so is to give her the freedom to succeed or fail on her own."

"If she wants to be a model, she will have to learn to work for it. It is a competitive industry."

"I hope you will not mind if an old man wants to come by the offices and visit occasionally."

Before Megan, Xavier would have refused. He would not have wanted interference or anyone telling him how to run his business. But thanks to his bighearted equestrian, he now knew that success wasn't about the money. It was about surrounding yourself with the things and the people who mattered.

"You will always be welcome at Alexandre-Debussey."

They shook on the deal. But Xavier's excitement did not come from becoming the CEO of the two largest privately owned perfumeries. The rush of adrenaline pumping through his veins came from knowing he was hours away from having everything his heart desired.

If Megan would agree.

"Stop the car." The words burst from Megan's mouth when she spotted a familiar shadow on her front porch.

Hannah hit the brakes, skidding tires a little in front of the cottage. "What is it?"

Megan's heart thundered in her chest and her ears like a herd of spooked horses. She lifted a shaky finger and pointed. "Xavier is here."

"The bastard."

Hannah threw the car into Park and reached for the door handle. Megan grabbed Hannah's arm before she could jump from the car and wage war on her behalf. "I've got this."

"Megan, don't be silly. The jerk needs someone to tell him to go to hell, and after arguing with my now-fired wedding planner for an hour, I'm feeling up to the task."

"Hannah, I love you for wanting to protect me. But I have to deal with Xavier myself. We might have to share our child for a lifetime. We have to learn to be civil." Hannah's mulish expression didn't change. "Think on the bright side. Maybe he's come to tell me I win."

There wasn't a snowball's chance in hell of that since Xavier never backed down, but Hannah didn't need to be stressing over this—especially since Megan had caught her cousin surreptitiously peeking at pregnancy test kits at the pharmacy earlier. But if Hannah had news she would share it when she was good and ready. Nobody rushed Hannah.

Hannah folded her arms. "I'll wait in the car."

"No. Go home. Wyatt's waiting. Didn't you say you had a special dinner planned?"

Hannah bit her lip, obviously torn.

"Go, Hannah. I can handle Xavier. If he gives me any trouble, I have the baseball bat you kept hidden in the hall closet for backup."

The bloodthirsty pseudothreat brought a hint of a smile. "Swing hard."

"You know I never give less than my best effort."

Gathering her courage, Megan climbed from the tiny two-seater and forced her feet up the walk. She couldn't even begin to identify the tangle of emotions cycloning through her. Only then did she notice the black car mostly concealed by the deep shade of the trees surrounding the cottage.

Xavier rose from the rocking chair and met her at the top of the stairs. He seemed tired and he'd lost weight he hadn't needed to lose. But he still looked good in his jeans and a silk T-shirt. Black on black. His pirate colors. And she needed to remember that, just like a swashbuckler, he was probably up to no good.

His gaze fastened on her baby bump with something akin to longing before meeting hers.

She stopped a good two yards away from him. Distance was her friend. "My lawyer says I'm not supposed to talk to you."

"Are you going to take his advice?"

She had the perfect excuse to send Xavier on his way, but her curiosity—and a tiny flicker of hope, damn it—wouldn't let her. "No."

But that didn't mean she'd let him in her house. "What do you want?"

"You refused to sell Belle."

"To you or your agents."

"What makes you think I sent an agent?"

"Xavier, no one offers that obscene amount of money for

a horse without having a veterinarian thoroughly examine the animal first."

He nodded, probably the only admission of guilt she was going to get. "Why do you want her? Besides to irritate me."

"Rocky misses her."

Her breath caught. "I sold Rocky to a thirteen-year-old junior champion."

"And she made a tidy profit by selling him to me."

The sinking feeling returned to the pit of her stomach. When Xavier wanted something he got it. "Are you trying to take everything from me?"

"*Non.* The gelding is yours. On the condition that you do not sell him again."

Her thoughts tumbled in confusion. "You bought my horse so you could give him back? I don't understand."

"You were right. Money is not the most important thing."

A part of her wanted to shout *Eureka!* But she didn't trust the contrite expression on his face—one she was absolutely certain he had never worn before. "Uh-huh."

His gaze dropped once more to her belly then returned to hers. "Do you still feel our son or daughter moving?"

"Every day."

"May I?"

She threw her hands up defensively and backed away a step. Her emotions were on edge. She couldn't afford to let him touch her right now. "Xavier, why are you here?"

"I came to tell you I have dropped the custody suit."

Shock and elation spiked her pulse rate. But questions rained down just as quickly. "I haven't heard that from my attorney."

He reached for his back pocket, withdrew a thick sheaf of folded papers and offered them to her. "It is all in here. I asked him to let me tell you."

She took the document, but didn't attempt to read it. She couldn't have translated legalese at the moment if her life depended on it. He had her too rattled. "Why? You never give up on something that matters to you."

"You matter to me."

Her heart and lungs stalled. "What are you saying?"

"That our child will be very fortunate to have you for a mother. Your willingness to sacrifice everything that you hold dear—your horses, your career—is true honor, and it shows me that you will always put our son or daughter first. Our child will never lack for love or doubt that he or she is truly wanted."

"No. Our baby will *always* be loved and wanted."

"I will buy you a stable of your own in the States or Europe. Wherever you prefer to raise the baby. You choose the property. I will provide financial support and cover the salary of the best nanny available so that the *bébé* can travel with you when you return to the career you love—riding."

A stable of her own had been a far-off dream of Megan's for years, but she'd never expected to be able to afford one. Xavier was offering her everything and more than she had ever wanted. "What's the catch?"

"There is none. You were right. It is not the money, the power or the prestige that matters in life. It is the people. I regret that my father went to his grave with me cursing him for bringing shame to the Alexandre name by abandoning what I felt was his duty. But he was not wrong. I was. He did not shame the family. He honored them by following his heart rather than greed. He married my mother and gave me his name. I cannot apologize to him or make things right with him. But I can with you. I am sorry for the distress I have caused you, Megan."

"This is a pretty huge change of heart for you, Xavier."

And totally out of character—so much so she didn't know what to make of it.

"I was—" His voice broke, stunning Megan. She had never seen him lose composure. His face reflected his struggle. "I was wrong. I n-need you in my life."

Emotions welled inside her, blocking her throat. She gulped and wheezed a breath into her tight chest. "You know there's only one way that's going to happen. End your engage—"

"I have. I am not going to marry Cecille. There is no honor in marrying for money or property."

Jubilation fizzed inside her. "And Cecille?"

"Is relieved. Her father and I have worked a deal. She will be the spokesmodel for Parfums Alexandre-Debussey and she does not have to marry me to get it."

"Alexandre-Debussey?"

"I bought the company outright."

"What about the Alexandre Estate?"

"You once told me a home is no good without a family to share it. The estate would not have been a home. It would have been just another possession. Debussey wishes to keep it for sentimental reasons. That was the home he shared with Cecille's mother and where he claims he was the happiest."

Something fluttered deep inside her—something besides the baby now kicking like a bucking horse. She reached for Xavier's hand and covered the little jabbing feet. "I think junior approves."

Xavier jerked as the baby kicked her stomach beneath his palm. His breath shallowed and excitement lit his eyes. "He or she is a fighter."

"Like his or her parents." She stepped out of reach so she could think, then took a deep breath and gathered her thoughts. As difficult as it might be, she had to do what was right for her and her baby. "Xavier, as much as I appreciate your generous offer, I'm going to have to decline."

"Why? I do not understand. I am offering you what you want."

"No piece of land is worth living without love or under a feeling of indebtedness. The only thing I've ever wanted from you is free. Your love."

His stupefied face would have been comical if she'd been in the mood to laugh about anything. "Have my actions not proven I care for you?"

Care. Not love. That hurt. So, so much. She shuffled backward toward the door, determined to get inside and tend her wounds in private before the tears stinging her eyes broke free.

Xavier caught her hand, his grip firm, strong and warm. "Megan, the stable, the money, everything I offer is yours with no strings attached whether or not you choose to allow me to be a part of your life or a part of our child's life. I want what is best for you. I want you to be happy. Only you know whether that includes me."

Her feet and heart stalled.

"I will not lie, *mon amante*. I would very much like to be by your side for the remainder of our days. To grow old and gray with you. You are the only woman to whom I can fathom making such a promise. You have the courage to fight for what you believe in. And I am hoping somewhere in your heart you have the capacity to forgive me for being such a blind ass."

Her lips quivered. She hid them behind her fingers. What he said was too good to be true and she was afraid to believe in the fairy tale again because she couldn't survive losing it again.

"What do you want from me, Xavier?"

"I want you to love me like you used to." He lifted a hand and cupped her face. "To love me as I do you."

She gasped. Tears puddled in her eyes. He'd said *the words*. The absolutely perfect words. But...

"This is not because of the baby, is it?"

"No, *mon amante*. This is because I am lost without you. I eat, work, sleep—badly—but my days are empty without you in them. Come home with me. Rocky Start misses you. I miss you, Megan."

She saw the truth in his beautiful green eyes. He loved her. Loved *her*. "I've never stopped loving you, Xavier. Believe me, I tried. I gave it everything I had and I failed."

His lips—the lips she adored—curved in a smile. "I rejoice in your failure. I have one more request, but you have my love regardless of your answer, *tu comprends?*"

Curious, she nodded. "I understand."

He reached into his pocket and pulled out something small, narrow, shiny and silver. He held it between his fingers and offered it to her. It was a band. With bas-relief turtles between the raised edges.

"The ring is platinum. The jeweler who designed it for me assures me it is practically indestructible. And the smooth edges should prevent it from snagging on anything or getting in your way. Marry me, Megan. Wear this wedding band on your finger and let us spend the rest of our lives loving each other."

Emotions overwhelmed her. Xavier was offering more than she'd ever dreamed of, more than a fantasy. A home. A family. A man who loved her as much as her parents had loved each other. One who was willing to travel the show circuit with her so that they would not have to spend long weekends apart.

"I would love to marry you, grow old with you and raise children with you, Xavier. Yes, I'll marry you."

Xavier drew a deep, slow breath. *"Merci, mon amour."*

And then he pulled her into his arms and held her, just held her, close enough that their hearts pounded against each other. He leaned back slightly and brushed her lips with a kiss so tender and reverent a tear slipped from her eye.

He lifted his head. Happiness and love glowed in his eyes.

Laughter she couldn't contain bubbled up her throat. "The ring is perfect. Turtles."

"Please tell me the significance of the reptiles. You have them everywhere. And while I would love for you to remove your panties to distract me, it won't work this time."

It was a secret only Hannah knew. "When I lived here after my family died and my uncle rode my case, I used to withdraw. Hannah always called it pulling into my shell. Like a turtle."

Alarm crossed his face. "Then the ring brings back bad memories? I am sorry—"

"No. Turtles are hard on the outside. They can withdraw and protect themselves when necessary. And then when the threat has passed, they move on with their lives. They're strong and resilient, and no one touches their tender core."

He threaded his fingers through her hair. "And you are very much like the turtle. Strong and resilient. *Oui.* I see it. But I promise you, I will give you no cause to disappear into your shell."

He kissed her again, but this kiss was different than any they had shared before. It not only held passion. It overflowed with love.

Epilogue

Don't cry. Don't cry. Don't cry.

Megan blinked furiously as she studied herself in the mirror of the cathedral's anteroom. She'd never expected to see this day and her heart was so full it was ready to burst.

"Stop that. You'll ruin your makeup," Hannah chided gently over Megan's right shoulder as she slipped another hairpin into the rope of pearls holding Megan's veil.

Nellie tsked on Megan's left. "Hush, Hannah Faith. It wasn't long ago you were crying into your wedding bouquet. Happy tears are always welcome. It's a body's way of making room for more joy. Here's a tissue, honey."

Megan carefully dabbed her eyes and looked at the faces of the women she loved, her family, reflected back at her. "Thank you. Both. For everything."

Nellie gave her a gentle squeeze. "You girls are like daughters to me. Megan, I'm honored to have you wear my wedding dress, and I know my mother is smiling down from heaven on you right now. You look absolutely stunning in her gown."

A vintage wedding dress—something Megan had never expected to wear—that had not one, but two happy marriages behind it. When Nellie had offered Megan her gown, Megan had been moved to tears.

Nellie patted Megan's rounded belly. "And maybe one day this little girl will wear it."

Her daughter. Hers and Xavier's. They'd found out yesterday when the doctor had done the follow-up ultrasound. They would start their new family in the New Year by welcoming a baby girl.

"Nellie's right. You look beautiful and radiant." Hannah fluffed the veil. "My mother's veil matches Nellie's dress perfectly. With that empire waist no one can tell you're seven months pregnant, and the beaded scoop neck bodice makes the most of your...enhanced assets. Cousin, I do believe Xavier is going to love your cleavage."

Megan's cheeks warmed. She stroked a hand down the heavy ivory satin skirt. "I feel like a princess. A very pregnant princess, but still..."

"I can't believe Xavier pulled this together so quickly." Hannah, her own baby belly just beginning to show, passed Megan her bouquet, a beautiful, lavish collection of Megan's favorite flowers.

"When something matters to him he can work miracles."

"Your wedding obviously matters. This cathedral, the reception at his estate, the horse-drawn carriage to take you from here to the reception... Megs, the man has a romantic streak a mile wide. Have you seen the flowers decorating the sanctuary? I'd say your perfumier knows his blooms. It smells heavenly out there."

"I take it you don't hate him anymore?"

Hannah shook her head. "How could I? He bought Haithcock Farm and donated the stables and the pastures to my horse rescue operation, and he plotted with Wyatt behind my back to do a major fundraiser for Find Your Center. I knew he and Wyatt were working on an advertising campaign for the distillery, but I had no clue they were doing something so huge for me.

"I'll be able to help so many more horses and disabled riders now. Best of all, he's keeping Haithcock house as a vacation home so you can visit me whenever you want, and our children will get to grow up as close as we were.

"But more than that, Megan, how could I possibly hate a man who makes you this happy?"

"Good point."

A knock sounded on the door. Hannah opened it to reveal Wyatt. The newlyweds shared a quick kiss before Wyatt pulled back.

"Showtime, ladies." He offered an elbow to Nellie. "As soon as I seat the most beautiful woman in the room, I'll meet the bride and her matron of honor at the other end of the aisle. Get a move on, ladies. The groom wants this knot tied fast and tight."

Nellie blushed. "Land sakes, girls, both of you found charmers full of blarney. But he's right. Let's get this show on the road."

* * * * *

PASSION

For a spicier, decidedly hotter read—
this is your destination for romance!

COMING NEXT MONTH
AVAILABLE DECEMBER 6, 2011

#2125 THE TEMPORARY MRS. KING
Kings of California
Maureen Child

#2126 IN BED WITH THE OPPOSITION
Texas Cattleman's Club: The Showdown
Kathie DeNosky

#2127 THE COWBOY'S PRIDE
Billionaires and Babies
Charlene Sands

#2128 LESSONS IN SEDUCTION
Sandra Hyatt

#2129 AN INNOCENT IN PARADISE
Kate Carlisle

#2130 A MAN OF HIS WORD
Sarah M. Anderson

REQUEST YOUR FREE BOOKS!
2 FREE NOVELS PLUS 2 FREE GIFTS!

ALWAYS POWERFUL, PASSIONATE AND PROVOCATIVE

YES! Please send me 2 FREE Harlequin Desire® novels and my 2 FREE gifts (gifts are worth about $10). After receiving them, if I don't wish to receive any more books, I can return the shipping statement marked "cancel." If I don't cancel, I will receive 6 brand-new novels every month and be billed just $4.30 per book in the U.S. or $4.99 per book in Canada. That's a saving of at least 14% off the cover price! It's quite a bargain! Shipping and handling is just 50¢ per book in the U.S. and 75¢ per book in Canada.* I understand that accepting the 2 free books and gifts places me under no obligation to buy anything. I can always return a shipment and cancel at any time. Even if I never buy another book, the two free books and gifts are mine to keep forever.

225/326 HDN FEF3

Name	(PLEASE PRINT)	
Address		Apt. #
City	State/Prov.	Zip/Postal Code

Signature (if under 18, a parent or guardian must sign)

Mail to the **Reader Service:**
IN U.S.A.: P.O. Box 1867, Buffalo, NY 14240-1867
IN CANADA: P.O. Box 609, Fort Erie, Ontario L2A 5X3

Not valid for current subscribers to Harlequin Desire books.

Want to try two free books from another line?
Call 1-800-873-8635 or visit www.ReaderService.com.

* Terms and prices subject to change without notice. Prices do not include applicable taxes. Sales tax applicable in N.Y. Canadian residents will be charged applicable taxes. Offer not valid in Quebec. This offer is limited to one order per household. All orders subject to credit approval. Credit or debit balances in a customer's account(s) may be offset by any other outstanding balance owed by or to the customer. Please allow 4 to 6 weeks for delivery. Offer available while quantities last.

Your Privacy—The Reader Service is committed to protecting your privacy. Our Privacy Policy is available online at www.ReaderService.com or upon request from the Reader Service.

We make a portion of our mailing list available to reputable third parties that offer products we believe may interest you. If you prefer that we not exchange your name with third parties, or if you wish to clarify or modify your communication preferences, please visit us at www.ReaderService.com/consumerschoice or write to us at Reader Service Preference Service, P.O. Box 9062, Buffalo, NY 14269. Include your complete name and address.

HDES11B

*Lucy Flemming and Ross Mitchell shared a magical,
sexy Christmas weekend together six years ago.
This Christmas, history may repeat itself when they find
themselves stranded in a major snowstorm...
and alone at last.*

Read on for a sneak peek from
IT HAPPENED ONE CHRISTMAS
by Leslie Kelly.

Available December 2011, only from Harlequin® Blaze™.

EYEING THE GRAY, THICK SKY through the expansive wall of
windows, Lucy began to pack up her photography gear.
The Christmas party was winding down, only a dozen or so
people remaining on this floor, which had been transformed
from cubicles and meeting rooms to a holiday funland. She
smiled at those nearest to her, then, seeing the glances at her
silly elf hat, she reached up to tug it off her head.

Before she could do it, however, she heard a voice. A
deep, male voice—smooth and sexy, and so not Santa's.

"I appreciate you filling in on such short notice. I've
heard you do a terrific job."

Lucy didn't turn around, letting her brain process what
she was hearing. Her whole body had stiffened, the hairs on
the back of her neck standing up, her skin tightening into
tiny goose bumps. Because that voice sounded so familiar.
Impossibly familiar.

It can't be.

"It sounds like the kids had a great time."

Unable to stop herself, Lucy began to turn around,
wondering if her ears—and all her other senses—were
deceiving her. After all, six years was a long time, the mind

could play tricks. What were the odds that she'd bump into *him,* here? And today of all days. December 23.

Six years exactly. Was that really possible?

One look—and the accompanying frantic thudding of her heart—and she knew her ears and brain were working just fine. Because it was *him.*

"Oh, my God," he whispered, shocked, frozen, staring as thoroughly as she was. "Lucy?"

She nodded slowly, not taking her eyes off him, wondering why the years had made him even more attractive than ever. It didn't seem fair. Not when she'd spent the past six years thinking he must have started losing that thick, golden-brown hair, or added a spare tire to that trim, muscular form.

No.

The man was gorgeous. Truly, without-a-doubt, mouth-wateringly handsome, every bit as hot as he'd been the first time she'd laid eyes on him. She'd been twenty-two, he one year older.

They'd shared an amazing holiday season.

And had never seen one another again.

Until now.

Find out what happens in
IT HAPPENED ONE CHRISTMAS
by Leslie Kelly.
Available December 2011, only from Harlequin® Blaze™